General Excellence.

JEWISH HOLYDAY STORIES

MODERN TALES OF THE AMERICAN JEWISH YOUTH

By

ELMA EHRLICH LEVINGER

FOURTH PRINTING

NEW YORK
BLOCH PUBLISHING COMPANY, Inc.
"THE JEWISH BOOK CONCERN"
1932

Copyright, 1918, by
BLOCH PUBLISHING CO.

TO THE MOTHER AND AUNT
WHO READ ME MY FIRST STORIES
THIS VOLUME OF TALES IS
LOVINGLY DEDICATED

CONTENTS

	Page
JUDITH'S CANDLESTICKS	7
A Sabbath Story	
A NEW PAGE	23
A Rosh Hashonah Story	
A BIG MISTAKE	43
A Yom Kippur Story	
HIS OWN SUCCAH	55
A Succoth Story	
THE COWARD	65
A Simchath Torah Story	
THE LIGHT THAT NEVER FAILED .	79
A Channukah Story	
THE BRAVE LITTLE OLIVE TREE . .	91
A Chamishah Osor Story	
THE PURIM PUSSY	107
A Purim Story	
A REAL PASSOVER	121
A Passover Story	
THE BOW THAT WOULD NOT BEND .	147
A Lag B'omer Story	
CLOTHES	159
A Shabuoth Story	
THE WESTERN WALL	179
A Tisha B'ab Story	

The stories for Succoth, Chamishah Osor and Lag B'omer have been adapted from the stories of the same name appearing in *The Hebrew Standard*. The Shabuoth story is an adaptation of a tale appearing in *The Ark*. It is through the courtesy of these two periodicals that they are included in this volume.

JEWISH HOLYDAY STORIES

JUDITH'S CANDLESTICKS

A Sabbath Story

Judith Weil was only four years old, but on a certain Friday afternoon she felt that she was a very big girl, indeed. Her mother had always insisted that on Friday nights she should have her usual early supper and go to bed directly after the Kiddush services, which ushered in the Sabbath, were over. But Judith's cousin Helen, who had come from college to spend her spring vacation with the family, had pleaded so hard in Judith's behalf that Mrs. Weil had smilingly promised to postpone the little girl's bedtime that evening until eight o'clock.

"I'm a great big girl and I'm going to stay up till eight o'clock," Judith sang merrily, as she trotted after her mother, busy with her preparations for the Sabbath. "I'm a big girl now, mama. Let me help chop the fish."

Mrs. Weil, moving quickly about the spotless

kitchen, shook her head. "No, dearie, it's all chopped and ready to cook."

"Then let me peel the potatoes—please! I won't cut myself once, 'cause I'm a big girl," insisted Judith.

"Cousin Helen peeled them for me," answered her mother. "Now run off and play with your dolly. Mama's busy and she has to hurry with supper."

But Judith was determined to help. "I want to cut the bread," she pleaded. "I'll make nice little bits of slices and—"

Her mother placed two freshly baked loaves upon a platter and covered them with a white embroidered napkin. Sometimes it seemed to Judith that on Friday night even the table linen seemed more white and fresh, as though in honor of the Sabbath. "But you know we don't cut the bread for Shabbas," she reminded Judith as she carried the loaves into the dining room.

"I know—papa breaks it off and gives everybody a little piece and he says something in Hebrew when he holds up the glass of red Shabbas water," Judith declared, proud to show cousin Helen all she knew about the Kiddush service, even if she just couldn't remember that big people called "Shabbas water" wine. "And first you light the candles in the big silver sticks. Let me light 'em tonight, mama, please, 'cause I'm a big girl now and I'm going to stay up till eight o'clock," she ended impressively.

Her mother laughed as she placed the heavy silver candlesticks on the table. "Not till you're married and have a home of your own, sweetheart," she told her. "I'm afraid," she murmured to cousin Helen who was arranging the knives and forks on the shining white table cloth, "that we'll never have a minute's peace, now that you've made her think she's grown up. By the way, what do you think of our Shabbas candlesticks, Helen? I know your mother told you about them."

"They belonged to grandma and she gave them to mama," interrupted Judith, "and mama told me a story about 'em. Once when grandma was alive," and she plunged into the story of the candlesticks, which had always meant more to her than even her favorite fairy tales.

She was still telling cousin Helen the story of the Shabbas lights when father came home. Then she broke off long enough to eat the supper which she considered the very best meal of the whole week; it wasn't because there was always special kuchen or twisted cakes with raisins; but, somehow, the lighted candles in their shining holders, the blessing over the wine and bread, and the songs which ended the Sabbath festival made the simple family dinner seem "just like a party." And to-night everything seemed more wonderful than ever, for wasn't she staying up till eight o'clock and didn't pretty cousin Helen not only put her to bed, but sit down beside her and listen to the rest of the "candlestick story" until mother called that she must turn out the lights and come away!

Of course, the next day was just as delightful as Shabbas always was for Judith. There was Sabbath School in the morning to which Judith proudly escorted cousin Helen, the weekly walk with her parents in the afternoon, and, last of all, the evening meal with its special blessings and the quaint old silver spice box, which Judith always sniffed delightedly before she put it away in the sideboard drawer and turned the key. Then came her special task of wiping the candlesticks with a soft cloth before she climbed upon a chair to place them on the mantlepiece on each side of the clock. It struck seven just then and Judith's sunny face darkened at mother's familiar "Hurry and push the chairs back, little girl; it's almost time to go to bed."

"But if you and papa go to the party, I want to stay up and keep cousin Helen company," Judith suggested politely.

Mr. Weil laughed. "I guess cousin Helen will be able to amuse herself." He turned to Helen who was helping Mrs. Weil clear the table. "I'm sorry we have to leave you home, but we accepted the invitation several weeks ago, and you wouldn't enjoy yourself with a crowd of old folks, would you?"

"Now don't worry about me, uncle Jonas. I've been having such a lively time going to parties and theaters all week that after I've tucked Judith in bed, I'll be about ready to go to sleep myself," Helen told him. "And it's about time for you to come upstairs now, lady," she smiled to Judith, holding out her hand. "Let me get you all ready for bed by the time mama and papa leave and then I'll tell you a nice story."

"About fairies," begged Judith as she hopped up the stairs beside her cousin. "And brownies and the fairy godmother and the three bears and little Red Ridinghood. Tell me all about 'em, cousin Helen."

"Do you think I'm going to tell you stories all night, you bad girl?" Helen pretended to scold her. "I'll just tell you about Goldilocks and the three bears and then I'm going to hunt up a nice book and take it to my room and go to bed myself."

Judith protested that she would have to hear

the story of Cinderella, too, and maybe the tale of Red Ridinghood and her grandmother; but even before cousin Helen had finished telling her the early adventures of Goldilocks, her lids began to droop, and, by the time the tiny bear was crying for his breakfast, Judith was sleeping soundly with never a thought of the other stories for which she had clamored.

When she woke up, the room was dark save for a broad ray of light that streamed through the open door from cousin Helen's room across the hall. Judith suddenly decided that she wanted to hear the rest of the bear story; she slipped out of bed, pulled her little pink bathrobe over her nightgown and pattered across the hall. Standing on the threshold, she saw that cousin Helen had fallen asleep without putting out the light, an open book lying on the bed near her pillow. Judith wondered whether it wouldn't be great fun to pounce upon the bed and cry "Boo" or growl like one of the angry bears in the story. She wouldn't scare poor cousin Helen very much—Judith had never been afraid of anything in her whole life— and if she woke her up it might mean the rest of the story. Then she heard voices in the dining room below; perhaps papa and mama had come home, she thought, smiling gleefully to think how surprised they would be if she ran down and kissed them. Or, perhaps it was company, thought Judith, some of the young people who were always dropping in to see cousin Helen; then wouldn't it be nice to run down and welcome them and tell them to wait until she woke up cousin Helen and told her to dress. Giggling with excitement, Judith slipped softly down the stairs and a moment later stood in the doorway of the dining room, blinking a little in the sudden light that flooded the room.

She gave a little gasp of astonishment at what she saw and at the sound one of the two men kneeling before the open drawer of the sideboard turned and looked at her. The third stranger who was stuffing the silver knives and forks into a great bag heard his cry of alarm and came toward Judith threateningly. But she was not frightened and stood smiling up at him; she was only puzzled who these strange visitors might be, for they wore shabby clothes and had queer bits of black cloth across their faces. And why were they taking the silver out of the sideboard drawer and why was the cross-looking man putting mother's best knives into his bag?

"Don't you say a word," commanded the man who stood over Judith, one hand still clutching the bag, the other threatening her. "If you do—"

"Let the kid alone," muttered the stranger at

the sideboard. "We can't risk anything like that. Hurry and finish and we'll go."

"But aren't you going to wait for papa and mama?" asked Judith innocently. "I don't think they knew you were coming—did they?" She seated herself comfortably, drawing her bare feet under her bathrobe, for the air from the open window was a little chilly. "And why have you those funny pieces of rag on your faces?"

One of the men had not spoken, but after a long look at Judith had gone on with his work which seemed to consist of prying open the lowest drawer of the sideboard. Now he said sharply and quickly: "She won't bother us; just hurry and finish." He turned back to Judith. "We're wearing our new caps," he explained gravely. "It is cold so late at night and these shields keep our faces warm."

Judith liked the man's voice. It wasn't so coarse and harsh as the voices of the other two men; she noticed, too, that his hands were long and white while theirs seemed dirty and discolored. She slipped from her chair and went to him, looking over his shoulder as he worked. "What are you doing with the lock?" she asked him. "You're going to scratch the sideboard if you're not careful."

"Your ma forgot to leave us the keys,"

JUDITH'S CANDLESTICKS 15

chuckled the man beside them, as he handed a silver fruit-basket to the man with the bag.

"But she wont want you to take all her pretty silver away," Judith told them gravely.

"Yes she will, sister," he answered with another chuckle. "We've been sent by the jewelry store to fetch away all this silver and have it cleaned." Judith could see him winking at his companions, but she didn't understand just why he should be so amused. "And she told us to get all the jewelry, too, and take it along. Know where it is?"

"She always keeps it upstairs in the dresser drawer," Judith answered readily. "But tonight she's got her rings on and her earrings, 'cause she went to Mrs. Kaufman's party and is all dressed up. And if you go upstairs you'll wake up cousin Helen."

"Didn't I tell you to hurry?" warned the man with the pleasant voice. "There!" as the lock fell and he pulled the drawer open. "I thought I could pick it. Help me with this truck, Mark."

"Do it yourself, Ben," returned the man who was filling the bag. "I see something else we'll have to have cleaned," and he laughed for the first time, but so harshly that Judith felt a little frightened although she hardly knew why. "It'd be like you to pass up the candlesticks by the clock and I bet they're worth more'n all the other stuff put together."

He crossed over to the mantlepiece and took down the candle-sticks. But as he was about to slip them into the bag, Judith caught his arm. "You mustn't take them away," she said quietly. "Mama wouldn't like it."

"She told us she wanted 'em cleaned," said the man, who had winked and chuckled. "Didn't she, Ben?"

His companion turned and stared at the silver sticks. "Shabbas candlesticks," he muttered. "I haven't seen any since I wasn't much bigger than her, but I remember 'em."

"Guess I'll remember to take them along," answered Mark and for the second time he seemed about to drop them into his bag, when Judith again interfered, speaking more earnestly than before.

"I wont let you take those candlesticks to the store," she said just as quietly as ever, but with a stubborn little frown appearing between her eyes. "They don't need cleaning. Mama cleans them herself every Friday night and if I've been a good girl on Shabbas she lets me wipe them off and put them back on the mantle. Grandma gave them to her when she got married and she says she likes them better than all her other wedding presents."

JUDITH'S CANDLESTICKS

"I knew they were worth a lot," the man with the bag told the others.

"It isn't 'cause they cost so much," Judith corrected him, very glad to have a new audience for her favorite tale. "But they've got a story. I like things best when they have a story, don't you?" she appealed to the man who had broken the lock, certain that he would enjoy the tale even if the others wouldn't.

"I guess so. What's your story?" he asked, continuing to empty the drawer, but in rather an absent way, his eyes never leaving her face.

"Once upon a time," commenced Judith, settling herself at his side and beginning her favorite story as cousin Helen always began her fairy tales, "once upon a time my grandma married my grandpa 'way over there in Russia. Do you know where that is?"

"My mother and father came from there," answered the man, but so low that Judith hardly caught the words.

"They were very very poor," went on Judith, using the words she had heard her mother use so often that she knew them by heart, "and grandma's papa had no nice present to give them except two candlesticks which his own mother had received upon her wedding day. So he gave them to my grandma for a wedding present."

"Hurry up," cautioned the man at his side. "Let her talk if it keeps her quiet, but go on with your work, will you?" But the man they called Ben did not seem to hear him.

"Grandma lit the Shabbas lights every single Friday night," the little girl continued. "And when grandpa got rich enough to have a store she liked them better than all the nice things he bought her." She paused impressively for a moment just as she had noticed her mother pause at this point of the story, then went on very slowly. "There were many bad people there who did not like us; they wanted to rob and kill all the Jewish people they could find. It was just Pesach—you know what Pesach is, don't you?" she demanded of the three strangers.

"Yes, yes, go on," answered the man with the bag, impatiently. He had dropped the candlesticks into it without attracting her attention and was now helping the chuckling man to empty the last drawer.

"I used to ask the four questions when I was a little boy," answered Ben. "I know all about it."

"It was just Pesach," repeated the child, "and some bad people started to burn all the houses where the Jewish people lived and shot them when they tried to run away. Grandma and grandpa were sitting at the Seder table when they heard the noise outside. They were scared and they tried to run away by the back door and hide in the schul where there was a big thick door and nobody could get at them. Grandma was as frightened as she could be, but she ran for the candlesticks and hid them under her apron. Then they ran as fast as they could and as they turned the corner—", again she paused, this time to ask impressively: "What do you think happened?"

"I can't guess."

"A man came up and stopped them. And he had a pistol and he said he would shoot both of them if they didn't give him everything he wanted. Grandma gave the man her wedding ring and breastpin and tried to keep him from seeing the candlesticks. But he pulled her shawl off and when he saw them—"

"Did he take 'em too?" asked the man who chuckled, interested in spite of himself.

"Of course not!" Judith told him indignantly, forgetting for the moment that he did not know the story as well as she did. "The man said: 'So you took time to bring your Shabbas candlesticks?' And he said it in Yiddish, just the way the Jewish people talk over there. And grandma looked him straight in the eye and said 'You speak Yiddish like a Jew and you know what Shabbas candlesticks are. You were a Jew once and should be ashamed to leave your people and try to rob them in the streets. Do you know what you ought to do? Come with us to the schul and help us and the other Jews there until the police come.' And she gave him the candlesticks and said: 'You are stronger than we are and you have a pistol. Carry these to the schul and keep them safe that I may light them again as your mother used to do on Friday nights when your father blessed you.' And the man cried—mama said he did, but I don't believe big men ever cry, do you?"

"How should I know?" answered Ben and his voice was husky.

"And he took care of the candlesticks for grandma," ended Judith happily, "and was never bad again as long as he lived. Mamma says she doesn't know about that, but I don't believe he was 'cause—"

Mark gave a low warning whistle. "Some one at the front door," he exclaimed. "Quick", and he led the way to the open window. Judith stared after him. "Why—why—" she began helplessly, but some one turned off the electric light and she found herself in the darkness, groping to reach her father and mother whom she heard calling out in the front hall.

It was hard work to make Judith understand

JUDITH'S CANDLESTICKS

the next morning that "the three men with the funny black rags on their faces" were burglars who had kept her amused while they robbed the house. She could not understand how they could be bad men for they had not seemed at all like the wicked robbers in cousin Helen's story of "The Forty Thieves." And she found it even harder to understand why her mother cried as though she were sorry, a few days later, when the mailman brought a big package with the two silver candlesticks. For Judith was only a very little girl and it was not until years later that she really understood the letter that had come with them, the letter she gave me to read the other day, when she asked me to write this story.

"Dear Madam," it ran. "Here are your candlesticks. I'm a Jew myself and when I heard your little girl talking I remembered how my mother used to light the candles and I felt pretty bad. I got the men to keep the rest and let me have the candlesticks. I hope you wont tell the little girl what I was doing. She seemed to like me and treated me like an honest man. I was until a little while ago and I'm going to try again."

No name was signed to the letter, but sometimes when Judith cleans the Shabbas candlesticks, she wonders whether Ben kept his word.

A NEW PAGE

A Rosh Hashonah Story

Through the open window Harry could hear the other boys of the Jewish Orphans' Home enjoying the play hour which came between dismissal from school and the "washing-up bell," just before supper time. His geography lay on the desk before him, conscientiously opened to the map of Africa. Harry had failed disgracefully in his geography lesson that afternoon and Miss Herman, his teacher, had been cruel enough to suggest that he spend his play hour in drawing the map of the dark continent. So Harry had obediently sharpened his pencil, taken out a sheet of map paper and his geography—and had spent a good half hour gazing out of the window, wishing that he might be playing ball or tag in the warm September sunshine.

It wasn't his fault, he reflected angrily, that he had failed in his lesson. To be sure, he had studied only the first five questions, but how was he to know that Miss Herman would call upon him for the seventh? Anyhow, he hated geography; they always expected you to learn the wrong things like the names of rivers—and how to spell them, too!—when the only thing you cared for were the pictures of lions and monkeys and black men with bushy hair. Harry forgot for a moment that he intended to be a street-car conductor when he grew up, and decided that it would be a pleasant thing to sail to Africa like the hero of one of his favorite story books, to trade with the black men and finally be elected as their king. Nobody would care if a lion chewed him up or a snake bite him, he reflected, not even Miss Herman, who pretended to like him and then kept him in on the very afternoon that he was to be first at bat in the schoolyard game. As for Sarah— well, he supposed she would cry and wear black for a little while as any repectable twin sister would; but he knew she wouldn't miss him as long as she had all the pretty clothes she wanted.

It had been just two weeks since Sarah had left the Orphans' Home. She and her twin brother had known no other home for the past six years. The death of their mother when they were four years old had left them without home and parents, but as long as the twins were together, they could not help feeling, as Sarah once put it in her funny grown-up fashion, that they "had a real family." Sarah was extremely proud of her active, wilful brother and never ashamed of showing how much she cared for him; but Harry, who like most boys was very much afraid of seeming "soft", especially when his sister was concerned, not only refused to pet her, even in private, but took an unnatural delight in teasing and tormenting the little girl, especially when the other boys were about.

"Here comes Harry and his girl," Jake Perlberg would jeer whenever Sarah would insist upon following her brother about the playground. "Say, I wouldn't call her a twin—she's a regular shadow."

Harry hated to be teased and poor Sarah never failed to suffer when he smarted under Jake's jeering. "You just go over to your side of the yard and play jacks or jump rope with the girls," Harry would command in a fierce whisper, "or I"—he sometimes paused to think of a very fearful threat, "or I won't speak to you for a week."

"Just let me sit on the steps here and watch you play ball," Sarah would plead. "I get lonely on the other side of the yard and I like to be near you."

"You do just what I tell you," was the stern answer. "And if you don't mind me, I'll run off and be a sailor or a soldier or something. And then you'll be lonely all right!"

But Harry was not obliged to run away to escape his sister's embarrassing attentions.

As he sat alone in the schoolroom that sunny September afternoon, a few days before Rosh Hashonah, he knew only too well that there was no Sarah waiting outside to sympathize with him as soon as his captivity was over. For just two weeks before Sarah had been adopted and had left the Home and her brother to live with Mr. and Mrs. Stern in their beautiful house in the suburbs. Miss Herman and Mr. Fridus, the superintendent of the Home, had both objected to breaking up the twins' "family." But as Mrs. Stern insisted that she couldn't be bothered with two children and didn't care much for boys anyhow, it had seemed best to allow Sarah to leave her brother. Sarah had cried a good deal and protested that she just couldn't desert Harry until Miss Herman comforted her with promises of frequent visits; while Harry had pretended very successfully that he was really relieved to be rid of "that silly girl" as he called her, and threatened to fight Jake, when that mischief-maker accused him of feeling "home-sick."

Perhaps Harry wasn't "home-sick," but he certainly missed Sarah. He wasn't very fond of her, of course, but he wanted somebody around who didn't mind his teasing. He knew he wouldn't care a cent for her letters, yet he felt strangely resentful because she had not sent him even a post-card since going to her new home. Well, he just wouldn't write to her, he decided, and if she got too lonely without him, it was her own fault.

The door opened and Miss Herman entered. Harry admired her secretly and was sure that she was the prettiest and smartest teacher in the Home; but he would not have let her know for the world. Only "sissies" loved their teachers and Harry did not want to be considered one of that despised class. At that moment he wanted to snuggle close against Miss Herman, to tell her he felt lonely and abused, but knew he was bad and was going to try to do better; instead, he scowled fiercely and when asked to show his map muttered: "Haven't done it yet."

"You had better do it as soon as you can," suggested Miss Herman quietly. "You will have to stay in until you do and it is almost supper time now." Then she went out without another word.

Harry tore his sheet of map paper viciously across. He wouldn't draw that old map, he decided, if they kept him here all night—no, not if he had to stay locked up as long as the man in the poem in his reader stayed in his dungeon. He grew quite cheerful over the prospect. It must be very interesting to live in a dungeon and make friends of rats and lizards and not come out until your hair was white and have people make up poetry about you to be studied in English classes. Which reminded Harry that he hadn't prepared his English composition for next week. He wasn't in any hurry to do it; he usually preferred the fifteen minutes before English for writing compositions, but now anything seemed better than drawing maps of Africa. He took out his composition book and scrawled the assigned topic, "Rosh Hashonah and What It Means to Me," carefully underlining the title. Then he stopped to wonder just what to write, for how could he tell enough about Rosh Hashonah to fill the required page?

"She said we were to tell first what it meant," he remembered at last, and wrote: "Rosh Hashonah is Hebrew; it means the head of the year. It is the day that begins the year." Another pause in which he stared at two happy flies buzzing on the pane. Flies didn't have to go to school and draw maps and write compositions, he thought enviously. Flies were in luck! At last he remembered another sentence from a talk on Rosh Hashonah which Mr. Fridus had given the children the year before, so he added: "Rosh Hashonah is the day for beginning things. If we have been bad, we begin all over again. We make resolutions to do right and keep them and then we are good and get every

A NEW PAGE

thing we want." Again his pen stopped abruptly and for a long time Harry sat with his elbows on his desk, clutching his hair with both hands, as he tried to think of something else to write. Suddenly he grinned joyously.

"Gee, it'll be easy," he told himself, "I'll just fill the rest of the old thing with good resolutions." He wrote rapidly: "It is a good thing to make resolutions to be good; if you don't, you wont know just what you are going to do all the next year. My resolutions are as follows: 1. I resolve not to play ball near enough to break any more windows, because Mr. Fridus says the next time I break a window he will take away my five cents every week until it is paid for. 2. I resolve not to spill things on the table cloth, especially soup. 3. I will clean my teeth every morning if I do not forget or don't have to hurry to get to breakfast on time. 4. I resolve not to fight Jake any more unless he hits me first. 5. I will study *all* my lessons. 6. I shall blacken my shoes every Friday and not talk during services unless somebody asks me something." He hesitated, then, seeing that there was one line to fill before completing the page, he added. "And I resolve not to miss people any more; it don't pay." He closed the book feeling unusually virtuous. "I'll copy it before Tuesday," he promised himself, "and maybe I'll change that last part, 'cause I really don't miss Sarah."

Miss Herman had not closed the door and now Harry sniffed a most tantalizing odor from the kitchen further down the hall: evidently there was to be hot ginger bread for supper Suddenly he decided that he didn't want to live on bread crusts like the man in the reader poetry; he preferred his regular meals. And, since Miss Herman always kept her word, it might be wiser to draw his map and take it to her before the supper bell rang. Whistling softly, he began to draw an object somewhat resembling a deformed mushroom with twisted lines wherever Harry felt like inserting a river.

Although he had written the Rosh Hashonah resolutions merely to fill his page, the more Harry thought about them, the more serious he became. Whenever Harry wasn't planning some mischief, he took himself very seriously, far more seriously than Max, who shared his seat at school, who always had high marks in everything and usually won a prize for good behavior at the end of the term. Harry did not approve of Max, whom he called a "regular girl baby;" yet in his more thoughtful moments, he couldn't help thinking how nice it would be to have everybody praising him the way they did Max, from Mr. Fridus down to the fat cook,

A NEW PAGE

who never allowed Harry to enter her kitchen. As though he had meant to upset a pail of milk the day he had rummaged the pantry for cookies! "Yes, sir," Harry told himself suddenly at the supper table that night, "I'm going to be good. I'm going to learn those resolutions by heart and stick to every one of them."

To be sure, in pulling the composition book out of his desk, he upset his bottle of drawing ink, which ran all over his arithmetic, earning him two demerits the next morning. But Harry was not discouraged. He tore out his composition, put it into his pocket and actually learned the first two resolutions before recess the next day. Unfortunately, his resolutions didn't cover all the bad things a small boy may do with the best intentions in the world, and during the play hour, while "shying stones" at no place in particular, he managed to hit and disable one of Mrs. Fridus's pet hens. This was bad enough; but when Harry broke one of the kitchen windows during a ball game the next morning, afterwards upsetting the gravy at supper and ending the day with a fight with Jake, he decided that there wasn't any use in trying to reform. He was meant to be bad and a hundred Rosh Hashonah resolutions couldn't help him to keep out of trouble and sail along as easily as Max. Even if he had to write a new composition, he wasn't going to be silly enough to pass in such rubbish as he had written a few days before.

He pulled the page of resolutions from his pocket, crumpled them into a loose wad and flung them toward the waste basket. They fell upon the floor, but Harry, wilfully ignoring the rule that no papers were to be thrown upon the schoolroom floor, strolled out to the playground. But he did not join the others in their game of stoop-tag. Instead he sat upon the steps and stared gloomily at a post-card he had received that morning. It was a picture of the public library and upon the back of it Sarah had written, "From your loving sister." Just that and nothing more! Harry felt more aggrieved than ever. He hadn't bothered to write to her, but then Sarah wasn't half so busy as he was, and, anyhow, letter writing was a girl's job. But this was all she had written since going to her new home—just a single line without even telling him she was lonely. Harry told himself fiercely that he would keep at least one of his despised resolutions: he certainly would not be foolish enough to miss Sarah.

That evening Miss Herman sat in Mr. Fridus' office going over the monthly reports of the children under her charge. The superintendent raised his eyebrows as he passed one of the report cards across the table. "Whatever have you been doing to Harry Mannheimer?" he asked her, with a half smile. "I put him in your division in June because I thought you might be the one person around here to do something with him. But now he has lower marks and more demerits than at the beginning of the summer."

"I wanted to speak to you about Harry," answered Miss Herman very seriously. "He's one of the best boys here—yes, even with an awful report card like that. Only he doesn't fit in as he should. We've made a lot of round holes for our children here, but Harry happens to be built square and sticks out at the corners."

"Well, we can't build a square hole just for him," laughed the superintendent.

"You wouldn't have to, if he lived in a real home. The boy needs a lot of extra care and petting and he doesn't get it here. He's been acting like a regular little demon this last week, but it's not his fault. In the first place, he just naturally falls into mischief; and then he's out of sorts and lonely because he misses his sister."

"I don't believe it. He was always tormenting and teasing her," objected Mr. Fridus.

"I found this paper this afternoon," Miss

Herman told him, as she took a piece of crumpled paper from her portfolio. "It was lying near the waste basket and I happened to glance at it before I threw it away. Now, don't you think he misses Sarah?" she asked triumphantly as Mr. Fridus finished reading the queer list of "resolutions," his face growing rather tender at the boy's resolve not to feel homesick for his sister. "She's the only relative he has and I know he misses her petting even if he used to laugh at it. I told you it was wrong to separate them!"

"But Sarah has such a lovely home," objected Mr. Fridus.

"Yes; but we're robbing Harry of his little sister. And I don't believe she's happy either." Miss Herman rose and began to gather up her cards and papers with her usual energy. "I'm going to call on Mrs. Stern to-morrow and tell her all about it. They can afford to adopt a half dozen children if they want to, and there's no reason they shouldn't take Harry."

"It won't do you a bit of good to see her," warned the superintendent. "She told me—"

"Well, just wait until I get through with her," smiled Harry's teacher.

She was smiling the next day when Mrs. Stern insisted that she didn't want to adopt another orphan, especially a boy. "I don't like boys and Sarah is all the company I need," she answered Miss Herman's plea for Harry and his sister. "Really, Miss Herman, you are very foolish to worry about Sarah; she is very well satisfied and as soon as she gets over her first spell of homesickness, she'll be all right."

"Then she has been homesick!"

"A little. That's why I haven't allowed her to write to Harry or go to see him. She's such a sensitive little thing, you know. Only he's not likely to be lonely. Mr. Fridus told us all about him: such a rough, lively boy wouldn't miss her after the first day or two."

"Mr. Fridus didn't tell you everything about Harry," answered Miss Herman. Flushing in her earnestness, she went on to tell several stories about the bad boy of the school, whom she didn't consider so very bad after all, just lively and too inclined to chafe against the many restrictions of the Home. "He's a dear little fellow, but he needs a lot of loving—the kind you could give him," ended Miss Herman artfully. "And he's lonelier than ever now that Sarah is away." She dropped the Rosh Hashonah composition into Mrs. Stern's lap. "I think he wrote it for a class exercise and then threw it away; I suppose he was ashamed of it. But don't you think that a boy who really tries so hard to be good is worth giving a home? And as for missing Sarah—"

"The poor little fellow!" Mrs. Stern interrupted, glancing up from the scrawled sentences with misty eyes. "Mr. Stern tried to persuade me to take him when we adopted Sarah, but I suppose I never took the trouble to think how much it would mean to the children to be separated. And the dear little girl has been too shy to talk to me about him." She considered for a moment. "I'll speak to Mr. Stern tonight, and if he agrees with me, we'll talk it over with Mr. Fridus. Only don't say anything to the children; it is no use to disappoint them, is it?"

"I'm sure they wont be disappointed," Miss Herman laughed happily.

It was Rosh Hashonah morning. Harry feeling uncomfortably clean and "primped up" in his holiday suit and new shirt, sat between Jake and Max for the children's services. Glancing sideways during the singing, he could see Sarah who had come in with her new parents just before the opening prayer. As he was already seated with his class, she could do nothing but smile a tremulous greeting to him before she slipped into her old place with the little girls of her class. Miss Herman's quick eyes had noticed that the child looked pale and considerably thinner than when she left the Home. But Harry only saw that she was

A NEW PAGE

dressed as beautifully as a little girl in a picture book; her white embroidered dress and hat with long ribbons made him wonder bitterly whether she hadn't come back for the Rosh Hashonah services just to show her new clothes. He refused to smile back at her whenever he caught her glance and relieved his feelings by sticking pins in Max, who, believing that Jake was the offender, kept glancing reproachfully at Harry's old enemy.

But after a while Harry threw away his pin and actually listened to what Mr. Fridus was saying. He explained the story that one of the older boys had just read in Hebrew and Harry who was never tired of hearing how Abraham was about to sacrifice his only son, became so interested that he was almost sorry when the story was over and the children turned their faces toward the choir loft, eager to hear the sound of the Shofar. Harry's heart thrilled at the long quivering trumpet notes. He wanted to be like those old Hebrew soldiers, who Mr. Fridus had told the children, gathered to defend their camp at the sound of the trumpet. Somehow, although he didn't know just why, he felt strangely quiet and reverent as Mr. Fridus put the Sefer Torah back into the Ark and drew the white curtains before it. It made him think of the great Book Mr. Fridus had said was just closed, the Book filled with the deeds of men for the past year. There was a new Book spread out before God to write out everybody's deeds, good and bad, Mr. Fridus had added, and today the Book showed a blank page. Harry wanted to begin the record right, he told himself, but there didn't seem to be any use in trying to do the right thing. Even Miss Herman thought he was a bad boy and he knew that Sarah didn't care for him any more.

Yet it seemed that he didn't care for Sarah, either, when she ran to him after services and kissed him happily right before all the other girls and boys. He frowned fiercely and, as he caught Jake's teasing grin, made up his mind to settle with him as soon as he could. And he continued to scowl even when Mr. Stern asked him to come home with them for dinner; anyhow, thought Harry, they might have asked me on a regular day "when I wouldn't miss anything here—not when we have ice cream for dinner." He remained sulky and silent until they reached the house, although he secretly enjoyed every minute of his ride in the smoothly gliding machine; he refused to brighten at dinner although there was chocolate ice cream for dessert. Perhaps he kept thinking how hard it would be to go back to the Home again, where instead of being a petted guest he was only one of three hundred boys and girls, all of whom seemed to get along better than he did. He did not dare to picture how lonely he would be there with no Sarah to smile across the table and ask him if he wanted more cake.

But Mr. Stern understood. After dinner, in spite of Sarah's protests that she wanted to come along, he took Harry about the grounds, showing him the greenhouses, which didn't interest him much, the garage with the three shining cars and the stables. Then Harry forgot his shyness and gave a cry of delight as he bounded into the stall where Sarah's brown and white pony stood. He threw his arms about the pretty creature's neck and snuggled his face against its mane. "I like horses," he told Mr. Stern," but I never had a chance to be with 'em. And I like rabbits, too. I was saving up for a pair of 'em but I never got ahead 'cause Mr. Fridus was always keeping back my spending money for breaking windows and things. Only I guess I wouldn't have had a good place to keep rabbits, anyhow."

"I thought of getting some rabbits for Sarah," Mr. Stern told him. "But I don't know whether she would know how to take good care of them. It takes a man to understand live stock, don't you think so?" Harry nodded gravely. "But you could help Sarah look after her pets, especially the pony, every day after school. I've spoken to Mr. Fridus and he says he's going to let you stay with us for awhile. Think you'd like it?

"Yes, sir," was all the boy said but his face glowed at the thought.

"He didn't say much," Mr. Stern told his wife later that afternoon, "but I think the visit is going to mean a great deal to him. I wish," wistfully, "you wouldn't think a boy about the place too much trouble. I'd like to have him for more than a visit."

"I think we'll want to keep him for a very long visit," answered his wife. "Sarah's been a real comfort to me and it ought to be just twice as nice to adopt twins!"

Meanwhile Sarah was rejoicing over the prospect of even a visit from her brother. "And, maybe," she told him happily, "maybe papa and mama will keep you here just as they did me. Won't that be nice?"

"Perhaps," answerd her brother, trying to speak indifferently. He felt that he couldn't tell even Sarah how much he wanted to live in a real home with a jolly person like Mr. Stern for a father.

"It's been just the nicest Rosh Hashonah I've ever had," went on Sarah, "and if you only didn't have to go away again—"

"It would be sort of nice to begin living here today," admitted her brother. "It'd be just like—well, just like starting a new page in your composition book. I think I'd like Mr. Stern a lot; he said he'd think about taking me hunting sometime. And I suppose I'd get used to Mrs. Stern even if she is fussy and like to live with her, too."

"And wouldn't you like to live here and see me every day?" Sarah asked a trifle jealously.

"I suppose so, as long as you didn't bother me to death the way you used to at the Home," answered her brother. "And I'd certainly be tickled to death to feed that pony every day. I bet Jake would never get over it if he could see me riding her!"

A BIG MISTAKE

A Yom Kippur Story

When Isadore Bergman graduated from grammer school, he planned to enter high school in the fall. Like many other fourteen year old boys, he had his future carefully planned and it was a rosy one. He would prepare himself for college, he thought, take a course in engineering and in a few years be building bridges in South America or China. It would be very lonely for his father who was a widower and had no other children; but Isadore decided that he would soon earn enough to take a real vacation and "show father a good time." Then his father would give up his position in the factory and the two would take a trip around the world, having no end of adventures, from shooting lions in Africa to fighting pirates on the South Seas. He did not tell all of these ambitions to his quiet, hard-working father, for, although the two were more like brothers than father and son, Isadore was a trifle afraid Mr. Bergman might laugh at his extravagant plans, and contented himself with hinting of "a rest and good times for you, dad, when I'm through college."

But Isadore never even entered high school. His father was severely injured while working at his machine; there were hospital and doctor bills which seemed to devour the little sum in the savings bank; and, toward the end of the summer, Isadore found himself with a bedridden father to support—providing he could find work.

It was not easy for the boy fresh from grammar school to find a position. He was too young for one thing and had no business experience. Besides there seemed to be a dozen boys for every vacancy. Again and again Isadore would hurry from one end of the city to the other in answer to an advertisement in the "Help Wanted" column to be met with the same discouraging information: "The position is filled." It was hard enough to hunt a situation all day; it was harder still to go home at night and chat cheerfully with his father as he prepared his supper and cleaned the two poor rooms to which they had moved after their misfortune. "But I'll get something worth while tomorrow, see if I don't," Isadore never failed to end cheerfully, while his father would always answer with the same heartiness: "I'm sure you'll get just the sort of position you're looking for, son!"

But when Isadore finally found a situation, it was about the last one he would have chosen for himself. Under the most favorable circumstances it would have been very hard for the boy to give up his plans for study and all the delightful activities of high school life to work eight hours a day in the stuffy basement of Barton's department store. He would have found the business discipline irksome enough, to say nothing of his loneliness for his old schoolmates, many of whom intended to enter high school in the fall; but what irritated him more than the long hours and the uncongenial atmosphere was the attitude of Mike Dorian, the superintendent.

"I hate him," Isadore told his father sullenly. "He isn't fair to me because I'm a Jew. I wish I could work in another department where he couldn't pick on me from morning till night."

"That's a pretty poor way to start in business," warned his father. "Maybe you just imagine that Mr. Dorian doesn't like you."

"Imagine!" Isadore fairly snorted in his indignation. "Why, he's been picking on me ever since I got the job. If he's got any extra work around the place, it's up to me to do it; if there's a single mistake made all day in the hardware department, he always calls me down without waiting to see who's to blame. I wouldn't mind so much if it was just because he didn't like me; but it gets me mad to have him nag at me all the time just because I'm a Jew and he seems to be the sort of fellow who hates a Jew like poison."

"If I were you," advised Mr. Bergman, "I'd do my work so well that he'd have to change his opinion of our people, even if he didn't like Jews. Though you may imagine he's prejudiced, I've known a great many Jews who were so thin-skinned that they always expected to be insulted on account of their religion. And usually they weren't disappointed! Just stop going around nursing a grudge, Isadore, and you'll not have any trouble with your manager."

Isadore remained unconvinced. He felt that his father knew nothing of the situation, that if he did, he wouldn't blame him for being thoroughly miserable. Disappointed and discouraged, Isadore was inclined to be unusually sensitive and critical. He even hated the other boys in his department, most of them were older and so much more experienced in business that they could not resist teasing him for what they called his "greenness." But most of all he hated Michael Dorian, the burly, loud-voiced Irishman, who bellowed orders through the long hot August days and seemed to direct his harshest criticisms at Isadore's aching head.

"You careless young Jew, you!" Dorian had

roared at Isadore during the first week when the boy had carefully stacked a huge pile of boxes on the wrong shelf. "Why can't you show some sense?" He had passed on raging, while several of Isadore's fellow-workers giggled softly. Isadore turned scarlet and longed to answer him, only restrained by the thought that his father depended upon the meager salary Barton paid him and he had to keep his place. But the words rankled for he felt that his religion had been ridiculed and any reproof or criticism that came from Dorian seemed to Isadore to come from a Jew-hater and struck him as entirely unjust.

Rosh Hashonah came and Isadore who had never attended school on the Jewish holidays stayed home from the store, taking it for granted that Mr. Dorian would understand why he was absent. But when he returned to work, he was disagreeably surprised to have the manager greet him sharply: "Well, are you ready to quit loafing and settle down on the job?"

"I wasn't loafing and I had to stay home," Isadore answered, rather curtly.

"Suppose you had to go to your grandmother's funeral—with a ball game afterward," chuckled Dorian with a wink at several of the older clerks who grinned dutifully at their superior's ancient joke.

Isadore's cheeks burned. He had often heard Dorian joking in his loud coarse manner with the other boys and they hadn't seemed to mind; but just then he felt he could not endure hearing this man make sport of his religion.

"My father was sick and he needed me," he lied desperately. He knew Dorian would accept his excuse, for the friend who had secured the place for Isadore had told the manager of Mr. Bergman's accident and at that moment he felt that anything was better than to have Dorian sneer at him for observing the holidays of his faith.

The twinkle faded from Dorian's eye and a hard look crept about his heavy mouth. He looked sharply at Isadore, but the boy's eyes were turned away and he did not catch the manager's keen look of disappointment, or was it disgust? Dorian was silent for a moment; when he spoke his voice was louder and harsher than ever. "You'd better decide pretty soon whether you're going to work for me or play nurse to your father," he almost shouted. "I'm not going to 'dock' you this time, but the next time you want to take a day off, you'll have to hunt a better excuse."

He blustered off, leaving Isadore to stare after him, hating him more than ever. The boy brooded over the incident in sullen silence, for

A BIG MISTAKE

he did not mention the matter at home, realizing that it was useless to worry his father. And now as Yom Kippur drew near, he grew more worried and uncertain for he realized bitterly how impossible it would be to explain matters to Dorian, to ask permission to remain away from work on that day. He laughed grimly at the thought; Dorian, the Jew-hater, giving him, a day off to observe a Jewish holiday! He'd likely not only "dock" him but tell him to leave at the end of the week. Isadore felt a little sick at the thought. He knew only too well that work for a young boy was anything but plentiful; he knew, too, that he could not afford to lose even a week's wages while hunting for another position.

"I'm sorry I can't go to schul with you this year, Isadore," said his father a few days before Yom Kippur. "It will be the first time you've had to go alone to the Kol Nidre service."

Isadore shifted uneasily in his chair. He had washed the supper dishes and now sat with his elbows leaning on the table, staring gloomily at the carpet. "I'll go to the Kol Nidre as long as it's at night," he stammered, "but I don't see how I can get away all day Thursday."

"But the other Jewish boys in your department—?"

"There aren't any. And I bet old Dorian

wouldn't let them off, anyhow. He hates us Jews, the old slave-driver; and I hate him," he ended fiercely.

"Isadore!" Mr. Bergman's voice had grown unusually stern. "It wont do you much good to go to schul on Yom Kippur to fast and pray for forgiveness for yourself, if you hate your enemy—or anyone you are bound to make your enemy. And, of course, you will stay away from work on Yom Kippur. I'll be sorry if they 'dock' you for the day, for we can't afford to lose a penny, but it can't be helped." And Isadore realized that so far as his father was concerned, the matter was settled. All night he tossed in his bed and thumped his pillow; by morning he had made his decision and was no longer excited and disturbed.

It was hard for Isadore to sit through the Kol Nidre services for his muscles ached from his long day's work and he felt even more uncomfortable in mind than in body. He felt a hypocrite as he turned the pages of his prayer book; what was the use of attending Jewish services and reciting Hebrew prayers, when only a few days before he had lied to Dorian, ashamed to confess that he cared enough for his religion to observe the holy days of his people! And tomorrow he would do something even more shameful, lie to his father who had always

A BIG MISTAKE

trusted him. For Isadore had decided to go to work as usual, telling his father that he was attending the Yom Kippur service.

He was bending over his stock the next morning, duster in hand, when Michael Dorian came down the aisle. He stopped on the other side of the counter, looking over the boy with sharp questioning eyes. "Why did you come down to work this morning?" he asked at last.

Isadore did not answer. Flushing guiltily he stood silent, his fingers tearing nervously at the feathers of his duster.

"I heard it was a Jew-holiday," Dorian continued after a moment, a rather unpleasant smile about his heavy mouth. "Funny you didn't have to stay home—funny your father doesn't need you again."

All the resentment of the hard, bitter weeks forced Isadore to speak, no matter what it might cost him. "My father does need me," he said hotly. "He needs every dollar I can earn for him. That's why I've listened to your nagging —and your jokes about my religion. And that's why I'm working on Yom Kippur and lying to him about it, too. My father needs my salary and I didn't want to lose my job."

"Who said you'd lose your job?"

"Aren't you always picking on me for being a Jew? Wouldn't you fire me if I stayed out

to keep a Jewish holiday? When I stayed out
the last time you said—"

"Sure." Dorian nodded emphatically, thumping the counter with his broad fist. "I wanted
to make you feel small and I guess I did it all
right. Don't you suppose I knew it was a Jewish feast of something, with my best neighbor,
Mr. Rosenberg, on the floor above, getting *yom
tov* clothes, as he calls 'em, for his wife and
kids and taking them to church! And I had
my opinion of you when you came and lied to
me like that and I felt like firing you on the
spot. But I knew how hard up your dad was
and didn't like to turn you out, though you've
been making me pretty sore with that long face
of yours. But what do you mean, anyhow," he
demanded with sudden anger, "by saying that
I got it in for Jews, when Abe Rosenberg and
I are like brothers, and Dave Goodman, my best
friend since I came to America, is a Jew, too!"

Isadore faltered. "But you called me a 'careless Jew' and—"

"All right. Next time I'll call you a careless
Chinaman, if you're that touchy. So that's why
you've been making a face every time I spoke
to you. Suppose I'm not polite enough, eh?
Well, any of the fellows around here 'll tell you
it's just Mike Dorian's way. And I will say
you're getting to be a good worker, only why

A BIG MISTAKE

did you go and lie to me like that last week about staying home? Ashamed of your religion?"

"No, sir. But I just couldn't bear to have you laughing at it and I thought—"

"The trouble was you didn't think." Dorian grasped Isadore by the shoulders and swung him around toward the locker rooms. "Hand me your duster," he commanded, "and put on your hat and go off and pray for me and your dad." He began to flap vigorously along the shelves. "Well, and what are you waiting for now?"

"I—I'm afraid I've not been fair to you," Isadore stammered, "but I didn't understand."

Dorian's blue eyes twinkled good humoredly. "Maybe I'll teach you a little about understanding the insides of folks," he promised, "while I'm teaching you how to keep stock. Now hurry along to your church and don't stop to play marbles on the way. They always begin early, my friend Rosenberg says, and he ought to know."

HIS OWN SUCCAH

A Succoth Story

"And the children of Israel built booths for themselves," continued Miss Feldman, "and they lived in them eight days. Who can tell me what we call these booths?"

A dozen eager hands shot up into the air. "Yes, Max?"

"A succah!"

"That's right. Now, how many of you children ever ate in a succah?" The teacher looked over the primary class and smiled to see the forest of waving hands, while a number of shrill voices added details:

"My grandpa always fixed ours!" 'We had a big lamp and—" "I hung up the grapes."

"Not so noisy, children! Now, I'm going to tell you all about the first succahs they built in the wilderness, and when you eat in your own succahs next week I want you to remember the story. So sit back and fold your hands and listen."

Thirty youngsters leaned back in their little chairs; thirty pairs of hands folded themselves in their owners' laps; thirty pairs of eyes turned toward "teacher" who plunged at once into a description of the long journey in the wilderness. Twenty-nine pairs of eyes, to be exact, for Harold Jacobson sat staring at the tips of his Sunday shoes, his brow creased with thought, careless of the trials of the early Israelites, as he tried to solve his own personal problems.

How was he to have a succah? he was asking himself. Harold was seven, but until a few weeks ago he had never known that there was such a holiday as Succoth or that some Jews ate in a booth of boughs for eight days every autumn. For there had never been any holiday observances in Harold's home and he had had no Jewish playmates until his parents had moved the spring before into the neighborhood where they now lived. This year he had attended Sabbath School for the first time and had become acquainted with Leonard and Robert Rubel, twin brothers with a wonderful mother who was always inviting their little friends to supper, and who never seemed too busy to entertain her young guests with games and stories. And Mrs. Rubel always managed to keep the Jewish holidays in such a delightful way that Leonard and Robert found it hard to decide whether they liked Succoth or Channukah or Purim best—they were all so jolly and mother made them nicer every year.

HIS OWN SUCCAH

"You mean to say that you don't eat in a succah!" Robert had exclaimed as the three boys walked home from Sabbath school the previous Sunday. "Why, I thought all Jews did. It's just great, and everything tastes better out there, and we always use an old silver cup my grandfather had for the wine, and mother tells us the finest stories—better than Miss Feldman, even if she is a Sunday school teacher. Say, Leonard, isn't it funny his folks don't have a succah like ours?"

"Maybe you can come and have supper with us the first night," suggested Leonard. "Mother'll be awfully sorry you haven't got one of your own. Last year she asked father's two cousins, 'cause they were away from home and couldn't have any and she felt sorry for them."

But Harold's quick pride was touched. "My mother was pretty busy last year," he explained, hastily, "so we couldn't do much for Succoth. But this year I'm sure we'll have one."

He thought about it all that week and now as he sat in his little red chair surrounded by his classmates, his heart was very heavy. Over half the class had raised their hands when Miss Feldman asked whether they had eaten in succahs. So many of the boys seemed to have had one, even if they weren't rich like Leonard and Robert. Why, even Myer Davidson had raised his hand with the rest, and Myer's people were poor and lived above their store and Myer often wore shabby clothes to Sabbath school. Then why would he have to eat his meals at the dining room table when so many of the boys and girls ate theirs in a succah?

Harold felt very unhappy as he walked home with his two friends, but he felt that he could not tell Leonard and Robert what troubled him. They might pity him, he feared, and he hated to be pitied. Perhaps, if it wasn't too much trouble, his mother might be coaxed into making him a succah after all. Usually he could coax anything he wanted out of his mother, if he kept at it long enough; unless his father said "no," which always ended his hopes. And he knew it was no use to appeal to his father, for Mr. Jacobson was always too busy or too tired out or too occupied with his paper when he came home from the office to talk to his son.

It was not without much stumbling and hesitation that Harold mentioned the subject that day at dinner. "Do you know it's almost Succoth, mama?" he asked, as soon as the soup was served.

"Is it?" asked his mother languidly. "Want some crackers?"

"Yes'm. And Miss Feldman told us how people eat in succahs. She told us all about it.

HIS OWN SUCCAH

Next Wednesday a lot of Jewish people are going to have a succah and Bob and Leonard are going to have one, too."

"Isn't that nice?" murmured Mrs. Jacobson. Then, turning to her husband: "By the way, Ike, did I tell you that the Delson's are going to have their anniversary dinner Wednesday night and we're invited?"

"I suppose you accepted."

"Certainly. Harold, why don't you finish your soup?"

"I'm going to. But can we have a succah Wednesday?"

"Didn't you just hear mama say that she was going out?"

"But we've never had a succah!"

"And we don't intend to have one." This from his father. "We're living in the twentieth century, young man. None of that old-fashioned superstition for us. Now, eat your dinner and be quiet."

"Yes, sir." The boy's tone was submissive, but the look in his eyes did not escape his mother. She scented further battles on the subject and wanted the matter settled at once.

"I'm sure you've got everything you want," she argued plaintively. "Yesterday I bought you that new painting set you were teasing me for all week. I never saw a boy like you— never satisfied!"

The child pushed back his plate. "I'm not hungry," he said gravely. "I don't want any dinner."

He left the room and his parents looked at each other helplessly. "I don't know what to do with him," complained Mrs. Jacobson. "He gets the craziest notions in his head, and he's so stubborn that when he once sets his mind on a thing he teases me till he gets it."

But it was not stubbornness which caused the little fellow to sit in his room, staring out of the window, his eyes brimming with tears. Nor was it entirely disappointment for he had never dared to hope that his parents would listen to him and give him what he wanted more than anything in the world just now, much more than the new painting set, which no longer meant anything to him. For only the evening before he had run to his father with the first of the pictures nicely colored, to be told brusquely: "Very fine; and now go and ask your mother if she's ready. I'm tired of going late to the club every week."

"And he never even looked at my picture," Harold had muttered on the way upstairs. "He doesn't care what I do."

Now he was hurt by something greater than his father's indifference. He was a proud youngster and he dreaded to go back to Sabbath school the next week and confess that he had not had a succah. It would be very hard to have Robert and Leonard feel sorry for him. Suddenly a bright thought struck him; he ran to the table where his Sabbath school book lay, eagerly turning the pages until he found the picture Miss Feldman had "told a story about" to the class that very morning. It was a reproduction of Oppenheim's famous drawing of a German family celebrating the harvest festival in their succah. Harold had built an Indian wigwam in the country the summer before. He nodded in a satisfied sort of way, closed the book, and, going over to the dresser, took his tin bank and shook it, smiling to himself as he did so.

It was near midnight when Mr. and Mrs. Jacobson reached home after the Delson dinner; but as they stopped in the hall to remove their wraps, they saw a light streaming from an inner room. Mrs. Jacobson frowned. "Katie is getting more careless every day. Just because I told her she might go out as soon as Harold had his supper, she left in such a hurry that she didn't even turn out the lights in the dining room." She huried away, but a moment later returned to her husband, a strange look upon her pretty, thoughtless face. "Ike," she half whispered, "don't say a word, but come into the dining room." He followed her wonderingly and together they stood looking down at their son, who had fallen asleep in his chair.

The little fellow had twisted bits of green tissue paper about the electric light bulbs, while around the table he had placed the family clothes horse, now hung with a green cloth and trimmed with branches. From the walls of this make-shift succah, he had fastened apples and oranges and one solitary bunch of grapes, the last looking decidedly "nibbled," as though Harold had been unable to wait for his supper until his work was finished. Upon the white cloth lay the remnants of the dinner Katie had provided for him, while a large tin measuring cup stood at his plate. Near his elbow lay his Sabbath school book and painting set—he had colored half of the Succoth picture before falling asleep.

For a moment neither spoke. The little lad stirred restlessly, and, obeying an impulse which he would have found difficult to explain even to himself, Mr. Jacobson bent down and kissed the boy before he picked him up to carry him to bed. Somehow he looked such a baby, curled up in his chair, his head resting on his arm.

Harold opened his eyes. Half asleep, he was not too self-conscious, not too much in awe of his father, to explain his triumph. "I wanted to stay up and show you my succah," he smiled. "I bet it's nicer than Robert's. I got the branches in the empty lot and I knew you wouldn't care, mama, if I took the green couch cover out of the library—I didn't get it a bit mussed—and I got the fruit with my bank money, and Katie gave me the cup. She said you'd be mad if I didn't put the stuff away before you came home, but you're not, are you?"

"Not a bit, son. Now go to sleep," said his father. The child settled against his shoulder with a sigh of drowsy contentment. Across the grotesque table the eyes of his parents met in a long look of understanding. Unconsciously Mrs. Jacobson turned toward the oil painting of her father that hung above the mantlepiece. "A worthy man in Israel has left us," the rabbi had said at the funeral. She turned to her husband with a choking little laugh.

"The funny kid!" She smiled uncertainly. "How it would have pleased father. He was always such a good Jew."

"I guess," grinned Harold's father, "that the boy's bound to be a good Jew, too, whether we want him to or not."

THE COWARD

A Simchath Torah Story

Ephraim had not been in America very long; in fact, it was just a month since his father had brought him to the public school and left him in charge of the fair-haired, smiling young woman he called "Teacher." Miss Amy had tried to make everything easy for the shy, awkward boy, but it was hard work. For Ephraim, although almost ten years old, had been sent to one of the first grade rooms until he could learn English. Many of the boys in his class could understand Yiddish, for the school was in a neighborhood almost as thickly packed with Jews as the little village in which Ephraim was born; but he felt a stranger among them. Perhaps he realized only too well that they all considered him a "Greenhorn," as they had either been born in this country or had lived in America long enough to speak and understand English. No wonder they gave themselves airs and were inclined to snicker when Ephraim stumbled over the simplest words in his First Reader.

But if the little fellows tormented Ephraim, the older lads were much worse. Sometimes boys enjoy teasing one of their number whether he deserves it or not, especially if he doesn't seem to have enough spirit to fight for himself. Ephraim was no coward; but he was too bewildered by the many strange things he saw and heard during his first year in an American public school, too ashamed of being classed with the youngest pupil, to try and defend himself. The petty tricks the boys his own age played upon him were hard enough; but it was even harder not to be invited to join in their games at recess or after school. To be sure, he had once been invited to "fill in" when a group of his schoolmates were playing ball in the empty lot across from his father's store; but he had been so awkward with the bat, that their hooting laughter drove him home, thoroughly ashamed of himself and determined not to join them again.

His old enemies continued to torment Ephraim even in Rabbi Goldstein's Cheder, where he went for his Hebrew lessons every day after school. Perhaps they disliked him here more than in the playground; in the Cheder he was no longer a "Greenhorn," an outsider to be laughed at for his blunders. For Ephraim had studied far more Hebrew than his American-born classmates, not only in the dingy little Cheder across the sea, but with his father who

THE COWARD

had been a cantor before coming to America. His father had also taught him to sing and was not a little proud to hear the boy's clear voice ringing out in the beautiful old melodies of the synagogue; but Ephraim had grown too shy and self-conscious to sing in Cheder, where the boys soon realized that the cantor's son easily surpassed the best of them in Hebrew. They might not have resented it if he had only been one of them; but it hurt their pride to have a boy, who came from the First Reader class in public school, continually petted and praised in Rabbi Goldstein's Cheder. If the good old man had only realized the situation, he might have made matters a little easier for his favorite; but Rabbi Goldstein, although a teacher for many years, knew much more about Hebrew than small boys. He was strangely unconscious of the fact that nearly every pupil in his school, from overgrown Nathan who was to be "Barmitzvah" in November, down to seven year old Oscar, never lost an opportunity of making life a burden for the "Rabbi's pet," as they came to call Ephraim. The boy tried to explain matters to his parents and begged to be allowed to leave Cheder; but his father did not understand.

"You are not used to American boys yet," he comforted Ephraim. "If they are rough, it is because you do not know their ways. Just wait and you will make many friends and like going to Cheder."

So Ephraim waited patiently, but he made no friends nor did he enjoy the hours he spent in the basement of Rabbi Goldstein's synagogue. Perhaps the other boys might have ceased to resent the Rabbi's favoritism and permitted his star pupil to live in peace, had Nathan only let him alone. But Nathan hated his Hebrew lessons and was glad to enliven the hours he was forced to spend in Cheder, by teasing the newcomer and making him as uncomfortable as he himself always felt when Rabbi Goldstein threatened to tell his father that he would never be ready to be Barmitzvah—no, not in a thousand years! Then the old man would often turn to Ephraim, and tug at his white beard and nod with satisfaction as the boy would fairly romp over the sentences that had caused Nathan to stumble. Which was very pleasant for Ephriam until he left Cheder; then he could consider himself lucky if Nathan was content with cuffing him or pulling his ears or throwing his cap in the gutter. But often the bully of the Cheder would be in a really vicious mood and Ephraim would go home sobbing with the other boys' taunts of "Baby" and "Coward" ringing in his ears.

"Baby" and "Coward!" These were almost

THE COWARD

the first English words he learned. He had come across the word, "baby" in his school reader and knew it meant a very little child like his sister Bessie; but he had been obliged to ask Teacher what "coward" meant. She did not understand the motive for his question, but she could see that the boy was troubled and tried to make her answer very clear to him.

"A coward is a man or boy who isn't brave," she told him, speaking very slowly for she feared to confuse him with too many new words. She considered for a moment, while Ephraim leaned against her desk admiring her bright hair and wondering why his mother didn't wear pretty blue ribbons around her neck and waist. It was recess and the big room was empty; Ephraim felt that he would like to come to school to Miss Amy forever if the other boys would only stay in the playground. "You know about David in the Bible?" she asked at last. He nodded. "David was a brave boy. But he would have been a coward if he had run away from the giant instead of fighting him."

"Oh—a boy who won't fight is a coward," concluded Ephraim.

Teacher laughed and felt she must begin all over again. "No. Sometimes it's a very bad thing to fight. You remember how I had to send Reuben home the other day for fighting in the hall?" Ephraim nodded. "But a boy is a coward when he runs away in time of danger." She indicated the picture above her desk, Washington crossing the Delaware. "I'm always telling you boys how brave George Washington was. I'm sure he wasn't always fighting with the other boys like Reuben; but when he had to fight for our country and our flag, he wasn't afraid and never thought of running away. Now you see what 'coward' and 'brave' mean, don't you?"

Ephraim nodded vigorously. "George Washington was a brave man," he said, looking up at the picture with shining eyes. "He carried the good flag and he wouldn't let anybody hurt it. But Jewish people haven't a flag like the red, white and blue one to fight for and wave when they march the way the soldiers did the other day." Suddenly his face brightened. "Yes, we have, too, teacher!" he told her, delighted that his people need not be behind even the Americans with their Washington and their flag. "On Simchath Torah, that comes next week in our schul, on Simchath Torah the boys in our Cheder make flags and carry them around. And the Rabbi will carry the Torah—that's a big roll of Hebrew with a red cover," he explained, "and he'll hold it like a flag and we'll all march after him. That's a flag, too,

THE COWARD

isn't it?" he asked a little anxiously, for he wasn't sure whether he was just right in the matter.

"I think that's the finest sort of flag," teacher told him, "and the Jewish people are the bravest people in the world. They've been called 'cowards' a great many times and some people think they are afraid to fight just because they haven't regular armies with guns and flags. But your Hebrew roll the rabbi carries, is the flag they've been fighting for all these years, just the way Washington fought for our American flag. And now tell me why you wanted to know what 'coward' meant?" She asked curiously, but Ephraim was silent.

When Nathan taunted Ephraim that afternoon, the old jeers had no power to hurt him. "I'm not a coward even if I won't fight with him," thought the boy. "I'd be just as brave as—as George Washington, if I got the chance." Yet even his talk with teacher did not keep him from feeling extremely miserable and lonely the next day, when Rabbi Goldstein excused the boys from their Hebrew lessons and allowed them to make flags for the procession in the synagogue on Simchath Torah. The other boys chattered merrily as they whittled flag staves or slashed at the pieces of bright cambric upon which they pasted all sorts of designs. Many of the pupils made their flags exactly like the blue and white banner of their Zionist club, with stripes of white and blue and a great star; others pasted gilt lions on theirs, copied after the lions on either side of the Ark in the synagogue; little Harry Rothschild, whose skillful fingers earned him the highest mark in drawing in Public School, chose a yellow background on which he painted what the pupils considered a truly wonderful likeness of a man with a crown and a harp, evidently King David. No one cared to see what design Ephraim followed, nor would any of the boys have understood why he cut out and pasted on his flag a rude, red scroll, bearing a faint resemblance to the Torah. He took it home with him and felt a little more cheerful when his father and mother admired his work; but he felt very homesick as he remembered Simchath Torah last year in the little Cheder across the sea. He had had so many friends in the procession of boys carrying their banners and lighted tapers; this year, even if his mates wouldn't dare to tease him with their fathers and mothers looking on, it would be hard to feel that not one of them wanted him for a friend, that they all shared Nathan's opinion and thought him a coward, merely because he never fought back when they tormented him.

THE COWARD

It was Simchath Torah morning at last. Every seat in Rabbi Goldstein's synagogue was filled; on the main floor sat the men and boys who were already "Bar Mitzvah" and had been called up to read the Torah; in the gallery were the mothers and girls and the very young children. For eight days they had eaten in their succahs and praised God for His harvest, although there were no longer farmers in the land of Israel, nor did they gather the crops of which they sang. But today they offered up thanks for the treasure of their fathers which they still possessed and cherished, their Torah; they had read from it throughout the year and now on this day, set apart for "Rejoicing in the Law," they read the last chapter and began to read their sacred book anew. Every face was bright with happiness; but perhaps no one "rejoiced" in the Torah quite so much as the small boys, who during the year seldom found happiness in learning to read from it. Now they stood in their school room off the synagogue, holding their gaily colored banners, some of them with sticks upon which they had placed lighted candles for torches. It seemed a long time to the impatient lads before Rabbi Goldstein, looking very tall and impressive in his long blue and white talith and carrying the Torah in his arms, came to the door and beckoned them to follow him. Then they went down the aisles after him, carrying their flags and torches, singing somewhat uproariously the song they had learned in Cheder. As they passed between the rows of worshippers, the men leaped out, kissing the red coverings of the Torah, pushing each other aside like eager boys as they struggled to be first to touch the Law.

Ephraim's eyes sparkled and his cheeks glowed as he sang with all his might. He felt like a real soldier marching in a great procession after his captain. For the first time it meant something to be "head boy" in Cheder, for on account of his high rank in class, Rabbi Goldstein had allowed him to follow directly after the Torah. And he couldn't help being just a little glad that Nathan was hulking far behind with the younger boys at the end of the line. For once he was the leader and didn't have to be afraid of the boy who called him coward and incited the other boys to torment him.

Suddenly the loose talith of one of the old men, who had bent over to touch the Torah as it passed, caught the lighted candle that little Oscar carried. A woman in the gallery saw the blaze and shouted "Fire," and, although one of the men caught the shawl and beat out the flames with his hands, the dreadful cry, "Fire!

Fire!" was repeated on every side. The women and children dashed down the steep stairway leading from the gallery; the boys in the procession crowded this way and that, some of them trying to escape through the schoolroom in the rear, others pushing forward to reach the front door, while the men and older boys, carried away by the general panic, sprang from their seats and tried to force their way through the narrow aisle, already choked with the frightened Cheder pupils.

In the mad stampede that had followed the first alarm, little Ephraim would have been swept off his feet, had he not clung desperately to the arm of the tall rabbi struggling before him, the Torah raised high above his head. Then a mad rush from the seats overpowered the old man and he fell to the ground.

The Torah was large and heavy, but as it fell Ephraim caught it and held it high above his head, as he had seen the rabbi do a moment before. He was glad now that he was not troubled with a torch to carry and he recklessly threw his precious flag aside. For he felt that now he carried the real flag and that he must not let it be trampled under foot. As Rabbi Goldstein fell, old Mr. Feldman, the shammas, gave a cry of horror and tried to raise the aged man to his feet. Several others assisted him and as they struggled to keep back the crowd, seething about the fallen man, one of the older boys pulled Ephraim to a bench beside him. A mad hope stirred in the boy's heart. He knew only too well that though there was no further danger from fire, unless some of his class mates dropped their torches, many people would be injured if the crowd could not be quieted. And if he were swept to the floor, what would become of the Torah he carried! Yet, why couldn't he make the people stop rushing about and trampling one another under foot? In battles, he knew, soldiers followed their flag, and didn't he hold the flag he had rescued when Rabbi Goldstein fell? "I'll make 'em stop," he muttered with trembling lips "I'll get there even if they step all over me first."

How he reached the Beemah in the center of the synagogue Ephraim never knew. But, dragging the Torah after him, he managed to climb across the seats and stagger up the steps of the platform. For a moment he stood there grasping the railing, almost sobbing with exhaustion and fright; then, raising the Torah as he had seen his father raise it in their little synagogue at home, he let his voice ring out in the strong, sweet melody that the cantor sings when the Torah is taken from the Ark.

The struggling crowd was shocked into a temporary stillness. The mad confusion ceased for a moment as all turned startled eyes to the beemah, where a frightened, whitefaced boy, his jacket torn almost to shreds, stood holding the Torah in his arms, swaying from weakness as he sang. There was a moment's silence; then Ephraim felt a great wave of relief sweep over him, as he heard his father's dear voice, far in the rear of the synagogue, take up the response. "Hear, O Israel: the Lord our God, the Lord is one," sang Ephraim, and, "One is our God; great is our Lord; holy is His name," answered Ephraim's father, and the congregation, hardly knowing that they sang, followed him.

"Magnify the Lord with me," sang Ephraim, his voice growing stronger and firmer as the men and boys, thoroughly calmed, stood quietly in their places and repeated the familiar words.

Rabbi Goldstein, white and shaken and leaning upon the arms of several members, walked to the platform. He tried to speak to the people, but the memory of what had passed and the horror of what might have been if the panic had not been stopped, overcame him. He could only lay his hand on Ephraim's shoulder, sobbing like a child. Ephraim, hardly aware that the danger was over, looked up at him curiously. Then, seeing his father beside him, he forgot that he was a brave soldier who had saved his flag, and, feeling like a very little boy again, clung to his father, crying hysterically: "Papa, aren't you hurt? Where's mama and baby—oh, take me home!"

But it was almost an hour later, after everyone had detained them to praise Ephraim, that the two stood on the steps of the synagogue. One of the older boys—could it be Nathan?—had lined all of the Cheder pupils along the sidewalk, where they stood at "attention," some of them still holding their torn flags. "Now, fellows!" cried a voice which sounded like Ephraim's old tormentor's, "now begin—" and to the boy's great confusion they broke into the old "yell" he had often heard on the playground and had admired, though vaguely, for he was never sure just what it all meant.

"What's the matter with Ephraim?" shrieked the boys.

"He's all right!"

"Who's all right?"

"E-p-h-r-a-i-m."

THE LIGHT THAT NEVER FAILED

A Channukah Story

"Father," pleaded Bennie, "please let me light it just once."

Mr. Roth shook his head. "Not today, Bennie. We have no candles small enough for the menorah; besides, you must not light the candles until the first night of Channukah."

Bennie pouted a little. When one is a boy of five, living on a farm three miles away from his nearest playmate, it is hard to wait patiently for a new privilege. And until this year Bennie's father had not considered him old enough to light the Channukah lights and say the blessing. "How long must I wait till Channukah?" he asked with an impatient wriggle, as Mr. Roth replaced the tin menorah he had shown him on the top shelf of the cupboard.

"Just two weeks," Mr. Roth consoled his son. "Suppose we begin to learn the blessing now?"

Bennie nodded eagerly and a few moments later his mother, entering the kitchen, smiled to hear him repeating: "Boruch atto—boruch atto—boruch atto Adonai—and what's the next word, papa?" She put away the jar of butter she had brought up from the cellar and stood for a moment behind Bennie's chair, her hand resting on his curly head.

"He learns easily, doesn't he?" she said a little wistfully. "When he is a little older, perhaps he can go to Hebrew school like his cousins in New York." She sighed, her eyes wandering through the window over the vast white fields. "It is lonely out here, away from all Jews," she murmured half to herself.

Her husband nodded, for he understood how she missed her family and all the neighbors in the crowded Jewish quarter where she had lived until her marriage. He realized, too how hard she found her many farm duties, how easily she became tired these days, when the heavy snowdrifts seemed to shut them off from the outer world and even the postman failed to appear down the unbroken road, bringing their daily Jewish paper and an occasional letter in his bag. But Morris Roth feared to return to the city, for the doctor had warned him that he would never be well so long as he worked in a crowded tailor shop. His brother had lent him enough money to travel west to take up a claim in Dakota; if he lived on the land just a little while longer, the government would give it to him for his own and there would be a secure home for Bennie and his mother. He had learned to love his new free life in the great out-of-doors; he felt he could not bear to go back to the city again; but he grew worried when he noticed how pale and thin his wife had grown, how often she spoke longingly of home. "When I have a little more saved, I will send her back for a visit," he told himself. "Perhaps she can take Bennie with her. If only her cough would be better and she would not get so tired!"

On this bleak December afternoon, Mr. Roth renewed the same old promise to himself as he taught Bennie the blessing for the Channukah lights. And yet that evening, as his wife moved about the little kitchen putting the supper dishes away, there was such a fine color in her cheeks and her eyes were so bright that Mr. Roth felt he had been needlessly anxious. But a week later she complained of pains in her chest and throat, and when Bennie wriggled because she dressed him so slowly, she allowed him to finish buttoning his shoes for himself. Bennie was thunder-struck; he was so used to having his mother pet and spoil him that now he just sat on the edge of the bed with his mouth wide-open, too astonished even to protest when his mother lay back on the pillows and said she was too tired to dress him. When

Mr. Roth came in from milking, she tried to laugh away her faintness, but he was badly frightened. He dressed Bennie as well as he could and awkwardly set the table for breakfast and heated some coffee. He would not allow Mrs. Roth to get up again, although he promised not to go for the doctor if she felt any better the next day.

The next morning Mrs. Roth tried to drag herself about the house, but by noon she was back in bed again, looking so white and weak that even Bennie was frightened. He stood watching his father with great round eyes as Mr. Roth pulled on his heavy boots and sweater, and moved nervously about the kitchen preparing for a trip to town ten miles away. Bennie went to the window and scratched a little hole in the frosted pane.

"Papa," he announced, "you can't go to town today. There aren't any roads. It's all white and smooth just like a table cloth."

Mr. Roth's lips tightened. "I've got to make a road, Bennie boy," he said simply. "I'll take a shovel along and dig my way through." He followed Bennie to the window and looked from the white prairies to the grey clouds over head with troubled eyes. "If the blizzard only holds off a while longer," he muttered more to him-

THE LIGHT THAT NEVER FAILED

self than to Bennie, "I'll get the doctor back here. But if we're held up in the snow——"

"Is mama very sick?" Bennie asked him.

"I'm afraid so." His father pulled on his heavy fur mittens. "So you must be a very good boy and take care of her until I get back. Don't worry her and if she doesn't want to talk to you, just let her rest. I'll bring you some candy from town and," with sudden inspiration, "if you're a good boy all afternoon, I'll let you light the candles and say the blessing tonight."

Bennie clapped his hands gleefully. "Tonight's Channukah, tonight's Channukah," he chanted shrilly. "Boruch atto Adonai—please hear me say the blessing before you go, papa." But his father kissed him hastily and started for the door. "Tonight, when you light the candles," he promised. "But now I must go for the doctor right away."

Feeling strangely frightened, although he hardly knew why, Bennie followed his father to the bedroom, where his mother lay tossing upon the bed. Her face was flushed and she threw her head about on the pillow. But she tried to smile when she saw that Bennie drew back afraid.

"It's just my throat," she managed to whisper. "I don't seem to be able to breathe.

But I'll get along all right till you come back," she ended bravely. "Just leave something on the table for Bennie's supper. And, Bennie, please don't come in and bother mama for a little while. Play out in the kitchen and let her sleep."

A few moments later Bennie stood in the middle of the kitchen, feeling very much alone. The rapidly rising wind howled and blustered until the frail little house seemed to shake before it; then the howling would cease for a moment and all would grow so quiet that it seemed as though he were the only living person in the world. The little fellow wanted to run to his mother, as he always did, for comfort; then he remembered that he was a big boy now, big enough to take care of mother and the farm, when father was away. He squared his shoulders resolutely as he went to the cupboard for his box of toys.

There were only a few playthings: the tin soldiers his Aunt Minna had sent him for his birthday, a rubber ball which had refused to bounce properly after he had pricked it with a pin, a box of dominoes, excellent for building forts for his soldiers, and several picture books. For a while he amused himself turning the pages and murmuring the stories his mother had told him so often that he knew them by heart. There was Golden-locks in a blue dress and red sunbonnet driven home by three angry bears; on the next page Cinderella rode to the ball behind six prancing white horses and here was Jack climbing the beanstalk which grew beside his mother's cottage door. Best of all were the pictures in the largest story book, pictures of a little boy named Joseph, with a kind father and wicked brothers, who stole his pretty coat and threw him into a cave. Bennie studied the pictures with satisfaction, especially the one of Joseph sitting in a big chair with a great many people fanning him or bowing before him. But soon he found that it was growing too dark to see the pictures distinctly; the short December day had deepened into twilight and the room was gray with misty lights, while the great stove in the corner cast queer flickering shadows on the walls.

The boy walked to the window to raise the blinds and again scratched a peep hole in the frosty pane. It was snowing hard, great white flakes that whirled and danced like bits of torn paper. Bennie shivered a little as he hoped his father would be home soon; he knew daddy was a big, strong man, but it was not good to think of him out there in the darkness. He wondered what time it was, anyhow. There was a clock in the bedroom and if mother was awake she would be glad to tell him, he reasoned. He stole softly to her bed. In the uncertain light he could see that her eyes were closed; she seemed to be asleep, but she made queer sounds like some one crying and her breast rose and fell jerkily beneath the blankets.

Bennie tiptoed back into the kitchen, curled himself up on the sofa and wondered what to do next. He had been taught not to be afraid of the dark, but he did want to go on looking at his picture books and playing with his soldiers. Besides, he was beginning to feel hungry and he was sure he wouldn't enjoy the supper of bread and milk and pie father had left on the table, if he had to eat it in the dark. But ever since he could remember, both father and mother had forbidden him to light the lamps. He wondered whether they would care tonight, when he was such a big boy, old enough to light the Channukah candles.

Suddenly he jumped to his feet. Hadn't father said, just before he left, that tonight was Channukah! Then he must light his candles right away, for hadn't father explained to him, while learning the blessing, that he must kindle the first yellow taper and say the strange Hebrew words just as soon as it got dark on the first night of Channukah? Bennie didn't understand just why he wasn't allowed to light the lamps, but would be permitted to light the Channukah candles; nor did he consider how worried his parents would be to have him striking matches unless they stood near to watch him. It was enough for him that it was Channukah at last and that he knew the difficult blessing over the light, every word of it. Why, he wouldn't have to awaken poor mother to help him, which relieved him a good deal, as he felt somehow that she would get well quicker if she were allowed to sleep as long as she pleased. But how could he reach the menorah father had put away on the very top shelf, next to the candle sticks for Shabbas? Bennie was not easily daunted. Even if he couldn't use the menorah the first night, he was determined not to be cheated out of lighting the very first candle tonight. He couldn't reach the box of little yellow tapers that father had put away with the menorah, but on the lowest shelf he found just what he wanted—an old tin candlestick with a half-burned candle which mother sometimes used when she went down into the cellar and didn't care to bother with a lamp.

Mrs. Roth always kept the box of matches well out of the reach of Bennie's active fingers, so he didn't trouble himself to look for them. Taking the candle he opened the stove door and thrust it into the flames. Walking very carefully, for he felt mother might consider what he was doing almost as naughty as playing with fire, he put the candle back into the holder and set it upon the window sill. Then, standing very straight, he slowly repeated the Hebrew benediction: "Boruch atto Adonoi Elohenu Melech ho-olom asher kiddeshonu bemitzvosov vetzivonu lehadlik ner shel Channukah."

Sitting on the floor in the warm patch of light cast by the stove, Bennie ate his supper, looking proudly all the while at his candle burning fine and straight in the window. When the dishes were all empty, he went to the window pane and amused himself by scraping off the frost with the kitchen knife. He wanted to see his candle throwing a pretty ribbon of light on the snow; he knew it would look nice, for he remembered how pretty the lamp in the kitchen window had appeared to him one night when they had come from town and had seen it shining as they drove up the hill. He wanted his candle to shine a long ways—just like a lamp—and, bringing out an old lantern which his father had once given him to play with, he set the light within it and again placed it before the carefully scraped pane. Then he sat down on the window sill, watching the snow flurries and wishing for father to come home.

Father came at last, bringing with him a tall, bearded man who carried a little black satchel and hurried into mother's room without saying a word. Father went after him and for a time Bennie sat trembling besides his Channukah light, wondering what it was all about. After a very little while, although it seemed to Bennie that he had waited all night, father came back into the kitchen and took the little fellow in his arms. Bennie saw that he was crying and it frightened him, for he had never seen his father cry before.

"Is mama very sick?" he asked.

"The doctor says she will get well," answered Mr. Roth, and his voice trembled. "You can't understand it all, Bennie boy, but there was something bad in her throat," and he added something about diphtheria which meant nothing to Bennie, who just considered it one of the big words grown-up people were always using to confuse him. "But the doctor has just burned it all out and she will get well. Only if we hadn't come in time——" He stopped and shuddered. "Bennie, if you hadn't put your light in the window we might have been an hour later in getting here and then the doctor says it would have been too late. Our lanterns went out at the top of the hill and the snow was so blinding that we might have floundered about half the night before we found the house. But your little candle helped us to find the way."

"I said the blessing all right," Bennie told his father, "but was it all right not to use the regular menorah and a yellow candle?" he ended anxiously.

"You did just the right thing," his father assured him.

But Bennie was not satisfied. "Please, papa," he pleaded, "please get down the real menorah and the yellow candle and let me light it and say the Hebrew for you. Please!"

Smiling a little uncertainly, Mr. Roth brought down the tin menorah and the box of yellow tapers. He gave Bennie one for the shammas, explaining that it was to light the others, and watched him with the same twisted smile as the child adjusted and lit the first candle. "Boruch atto Adonoi," began Bennie proudly, and he wondered why his father hid his face in his hands and started to cry all over again.

THE BRAVE LITTLE OLIVE TREE

A Chamishah Osor Story

It was many, many years ago, long before you and I were born. In the land of Palestine, across the blue waters, dwelt Joshua the Benjaminite and his wife, Shoshanah, and little Gideon, who was their only child. The boy was born on Chamishah Osor, the New Year of the Trees, and on that day his father planted a little olive tree beside the door of his house and marked it with a stone. And on the stone Joshua carved the name of his son and the day of his birth, smiling to think how the child and the tree would grow together, year by year, in the pleasant land of Israel.

Gideon was a fine, sturdy little fellow, with a merry laugh and an active brown body that never seemed to tire. But when sunset came, he was willing to rest with his mother beside the door of their home and listen to her stories of their people: of Moses, who gave the Law unto Israel; of Elijah, the prophet, and King Solomon, who ruled not only the sons of men, but even the birds and the beasts and the demons of the air. Gideon loved these stories well; but he loved even better the tales of the heroes of Israel: Samson, the slayer of thousands, and fair-haired David with his harp, and, best of all, Gideon, that man of valor, whose name he bore.

"O! mother," little Gideon would cry, "when will I wear a sword and a shield and fight the battles of the Lord?"

"When you are grown to be a man, my son," his mother would always answer, sighing a little, for he was her only child and she knew that she would be very lonely when he no longer played before her door.

But Gideon, laughing, would run to measure himself beside the little olive tree. "See, mother," he would rejoice, "I am almost a hands-breadth taller than when father made this last notch above my head. Surely, I am almost a man." Then his mother would smile at his childish pride, and it seemed that the little olive tree laughed with him, although it may have been nothing more than the evening wind stirring among the leaves.

"I am almost ready to bear fruit," thought the olive tree one day, "while my little brother is still a child. But he grows taller and stronger every spring, and some day he will leave my shade to do great deeds in the land. Then I shall be lonely to hear his merry laugh and I will find the days very long until he returns to his mother and to me."

The years passed and Gideon left his father's house, but not to wear a sword and a shield and to do battle for the God of Israel. The little olive tree did not understand what had happened: the band of fierce, dark men upon horses, the clashing of spears, the tossing of fiery brands, which left the houses of Joshua the Benjaminite and his neighbors black and smoldering ruins. Nor did the olive tree understand why, when Joshua fell upon the grass, bleeding from many wounds, the horsemen bound Shoshanah and little Gideon and took them away with them, along with other weeping women and children whose tiny hands were too weak to wield a sword.

But as the invaders began to move slowly down the long road, Gideon broke from his captors and threw himself at the foot of his olive tree. "I will not go away—this is my home—I will not go away," he cried again and again in his grief. The soldiers dragged him off, and the olive tree shivered to hear his little brother's wild sobbing. "But you will come again," he rustled bravely, or was it only the wind among the leaves? "You will come back again and be happy in the land of Israel."

The years passed and still the land was desolate. The olive tree grew in stature and in beauty and more than one traveler, pausing by the roadside, ate of its fruit and thanked in his heart the man who had planted it. But Gideon never came, and sometimes at sunset the green-gray branches of the olive tree sighed sadly, for the heart of the tree was lonely for its little friend. At such moments the happy past seemed little more than a dream, and the olive tree would have doubted that Gideon had ever lived, if it had not been for the moss-covered stone at its foot.

Yet the olive tree did not lose hope, for it had a brave heart and it felt that the little brother it loved must come back some day to live in the land of his fathers. The winter frosts chilled it, the summer suns scorched the silvery sheen of its leaves, yet the heart of the olive tree never despaired, but waited for Gideon to return. "He will be the same little child," said the olive tree, "for the sons of men do not grow old so swiftly as the trees. I wonder whether he will still be round-faced and bright-eyed; I wonder whether he will still laugh as merrily as a little brook in the spring time?" So the olive tree dreamed on, never realizing how very short are the days of a man's life, never knowing that Gideon had grown an old man and had died in exile in a far away

THE BRAVE LITTLE OLIVE TREE 95

country and that his children and their children after them were scattered over the earth.

Then one spring morning, after many centuries had passed with their burdens of winter frosts and summer sun, two Arabs paused beside the olive tree. One of them carried something shining and sharp like a sword, and the olive tree wondered dreamily whether Gideon would come back wearing his sword and shining breast plate. But it was an ax that the Arab carried, and, even as it dreamed, the olive tree felt the cruel steel hacking and tearing its gnarled trunk. The olive tree lay upon the ground crushed and broken, and the Arabs gathered up the trunk and the branches and carried them to the market place upon the coast.

"Alas, they are tearing me away from the land of my birth," sobbed the olive tree, "even as they took my little brother. Will I never raise my branches to the blue skies of Palestine again?" Yet, somehow, the tree did not despair, although it suffered cruelly when men cut it into many pieces and hacked and carved them into fantastic shapes. The beauty of the olive tree was lost forever; its silvery leaves were withered; it was broken as an earthen vessel breaks when it falls upon a stone: yet the bit of the tree that held its brave heart beat on as hopefully as before. "They have destroyed me in my strength; but my little brother will play again beneath the trees of Eretz Israel," murmured the heart of the exiled olive tree.

In the dark chest where it lay, the bit of olive wood could not know that it was being carried across the great blue water to a land of mighty towers and roaring streets, a land where many men dwell together in cities and sometimes seem to forget their friends, the trees. It lay in the dark, dreaming, hoping, almost asleep, until it felt thrilled beneath the soft touch of a child's hand. And the heart of the olive tree leaped in joy, for never since that dreadful day when his little brother had been torn from his home had the olive tree felt the touch of a child's soft fingers.

In the city of mighty towers and roaring streets, far away from the land of Israel, lived a little boy with a merry laugh and an active body that never seemed to tire. Like a great many other little boys, Judah loved to run and play; but often, when he grew tired around bedtime, he liked to climb into his grandfather's lap, resting his rosy face against the old man's long white beard, as he listened to the stories his grandfather told him of the heroes of their people: Samson, the strong warrior and fair-haired David and Gideon with his spear and shining shield. Little Judah loved these stories with all his heart and sometimes he would interrupt his grandfather, crying: "Grandfather, when I grow up, I will take a big ship and go straight across the water to Eretz Israel and see the places where all these people lived!"

"But the land is a long way off," his grandfather would always warn him, "and it is so long since we planted our trees and tended our flocks there, that sometimes it seems like a dream."

One winter day when the wind piled great drifts of snow in the strangely silent streets, little Judah and a number of other boys and girls sat in the big assembly room of their Hebrew School and listened eagerly while the teacher explained the pictures thrown upon a screen. He showed them pictures of far-off Palestine, the rugged mountains and the stately cedars, the tomb of Rachel, the gentle mother of Joseph, and the broken Wall where every Friday night our people weep and pray on the ruins of our Temple. He showed them lonely travelers bearing burdens and driving their patient donkeys before them, crowded market places and fair groves of olive trees. And little Judah sat with wide-stretched eyes, for he seemed to see for the first time the land which grandfather's stories had made so real to him. He decided that he liked best the pictures of the farmers working in their fields and orchards. Then he heard the wind dashing the snow against the window panes and he smiled a little to hear the teacher say: "It is not winter now in the land of Palestine. Two weeks from today, the colonists in Eretz Israel will be celebrating Chamishah Osor b'Shevat, the New Year of the Trees. On that day the farmers go into the fields and bless the trees. You see, it is an old Jewish belief that just as God judges the Jewish people on their Rosh Hashonah, He judges every tree on Chamishah Osor. A great many trees are planted on that day; then it used to be a pretty custom in Palestine to plant a tree when a little child was born. Don't you think it must have been nice to celebrate your birthday with your own tree every year?"

The teacher went on telling the children how even in New York when Chamishah Osor comes to us in the midst of the winter weather and few children have a bit of ground where they can plant even a flower, Jewish children can still keep the New Year of the Trees. "Next week," he said, "I am going to show you more pictures of Palestine and on Chamishah Osor we will have a little party, when each of you will

THE BRAVE LITTLE OLIVE TREE

have a taste of some fruit I am expecting from Jaffa—oranges and dates and pomegranates." Then, smiling at their eager applause, he tapped his bell for dismissal and the boys and girls marched down the long aisles.

Judah walked home slowly along the snowy streets, the sleety wind making his round cheeks rosier than ever and nipping his ears and nose. But he did not think of the cold; he was seeing again the wonderful land of Palestine where it was spring and boys and girls were planting trees under the blue skies. "I wish I could see and feel something that came from there," thought Judah, "instead of just pictures."

The next week Judah could hardly wait for the regular Hebrew lesson to be over, that he might go down to the assembly room for the new pictures of Palestine. Again he saw the orchards and the vineyards, the long winding roads with the olive trees on either side. "I wish I could touch those trees just once," thought Judah wistfully.

That evening he perched himself upon grandfather's knee to tell him about the pictures. "I used to think Eretz Israel was just a sort of make-believe country like the places you read about in fairy stories," confessed Judah. "But when I saw all those lovely trees and the high mountains, I knew that it was a real place with real people living there. Did you ever see anybody who had been in Eretz Israel, grandfather?"

Grandfather nodded smilingly. "Yes, indeed. I was going to surprise you; but perhaps it will be more fun for you to know now and look forward to meeting him. The son of an old friend of mine has been traveling in the East for the last two years. Yesterday he wrote me that he had reached New York and would come to see us soon. And because I know how much you love to hear about Palestine I told him to bring us some of the curious things that he had picked up in his travels and to be ready to tell you many stories. You will like that, won't you, sonny?"

"I bet he won't tell better ones than you," Judah assured his grandfather stoutly. "But I do want to see him—quick! Will he come tomorrow, grandfather?"

It seemed to Judah that the traveler would never come, but about a week later when the little boy came home from school, he found a stranger in the sitting room talking to his grandfather, a tall, tanned young man with broad shoulders and keen, black eyes. Grandfather broke off in the middle of a sentence to send a welcoming smile in Judah's direction.

THE BRAVE LITTLE OLIVE TREE 101

"Here is Judah now," he said to his guest. "Judah, Mr. Abrams has been waiting for you to come home from school. Now sit down and ask him all the questions you want about Palestine."

"I can't promise to answer all of them," smiled the young man.

"I don't want to hear him talk," said Judah rather impolitely. "But I want to see all the things he's brought from Palestine—not pictures, but real things that came from there."

Mr. Abrams laughed. "You're like my little nephew," he told Judah. "He hadn't seen me for a long time, but as soon as I landed, instead of kissing me like a nice boy and telling me he was glad to see me, he said; 'What did you bring me, Uncle?'"

"Huh," said Judah, unabashed, "I don't blame him. I don't like kissing either. Say, is it the way my teacher at Hebrew School said—that they're planting trees in Palestine now while it's cold and snowy here in New York?"

"Yes. Last year I was in the colony of Petach Tikvah (door of hope), and at Chamishah Osor—that's the New Year of the Trees, you know—"

"Oh, I know all about that; I saw the pictures. But did you taste the real fruit?"

"Of course I did and it tasted mighty good.

California oranges may be all right, but how about these?" Mr. Abrams pushed a box toward him. "I wouldn't let your grandfather open it until you came. Now you can go back to your Hebrew School and tell them all that you saw and smelled and tasted oranges that grew in Eretz Israel."

Judah opened the box, his eyes growing larger as he saw the golden oranges, the dates and the pomegranates. And there were queer black things, too, something like pods, which he was sure wouldn't taste half so nice as the other fruit. "What are these?" he asked, gingerly picking up one of the pods.

"The fruit of the carob tree. It's dried and ground and made into bread. I saw a great many carob trees in Palestine and although they are not as beautiful as the cedars and olives, I always like to look at them because they make me think of the story of Rabbi Choni. Has your grandpa ever told you about him and his carob tree?"

"I told you Mr. Abrams could tell you a great many more stories than I know," grandfather told Judah in a teasing aside.

"Please tell me about him," begged Judah, forgetting what he had told Mr. Abrams a few moments before. "Did he live in Palestine?"

"Oh yes, only a great many years ago," an-

THE BRAVE LITTLE OLIVE TREE 103

swered Mr. Abrams, while Judah after a nod of permission from grandfather, began to peel his orange. "Now one day Rabbi Choni happened to pass the house of an old neighbor and found him on his knees planting a carob tree beside the door. This surprised Rabbi Choni, for he knew that carob trees do not bear fruit for a very long time, and he said: 'Friend, why are you planting a carob tree? You are an old man and will never live to taste its fruit.'

"But the neighbor answered that he did not plant the carob tree for himself. He said that he had enjoyed eating the fruit of the trees that his own grandfather and father had planted in their day and that he was anxious to plant a tree which his sons and their children might enjoy. Rabbi Choni laughed at him and said he was foolish to think so far ahead. 'We are both old men,' he said, 'and soon we will be forgotten, for neither of us will live to see the carob tree bear fruit.' Then Rabbi Choni went on his way, but he grew so tired that he had to lie down by the road and go to sleep." Mr. Abrams stopped with a little twinkle in his eyes. "Did you ever hear of a man falling asleep for a great many years?" he asked. Judah nodded gravely. "Of course. There was Rip Van Winkle. He went to sleep in the Catskill Mountains—we passed them last summer when we went down the Hudson River and papa told me all about him. He slept for twenty years; maybe Rabbi Choni didn't sleep so long?" he ended seriously.

"Much longer—just seventy years. When he awoke, he was surprised to see the sun setting although it had been only noon when he had fallen asleep. 'What a long nap I've had,' he said, and started to walk home. But he had a hard time to find the road again, because a great hedge of thorns had grown up about him that noboby might know where he was sleeping. As he went down the road he met many people, but they were all strangers and he was puzzled when they looked at him queerly and stroked their beards. He looked down and saw that his beard had grown almost to his knees!"

"Just like Rip Van Winkle," murmured Judah.

"Even the houses along the way seemed strange to him," continued Mr. Abrams. "But at last he saw a house that he was sure he knew: the house of his old neighbor, the last man he had seen before falling asleep. He was more bewildered than ever now, for he saw a fine carob tree growing beside the door. A young man stood under it gathering the fruit and Choni asked him to call out his old neighbor. The young man stared at Rabbi Choni and told him that his grandfather had been dead for many years. 'But we have never forgotten him,' he said, 'for he was a good man and always thought of others. Why, just before he died, he planted this carob tree; whenever I gather the fruit I think of my good old grandfather.' And then Rabbi Choni knew that because of his selfishness, he had been allowed to sleep until he could see the carob tree bearing fruit."

"I like that story," said Judah critically. "I want you to tell me a great many more; but first show me what you've got in that other box, please!"

"Judah!" scolded grandfather, but Mr. Abrams only laughed at his impatience, as he opened the box and spread the contents upon the table before the eager child. He brought out bits of rare lace and silver filigree that he said had been made by pupils of the Bezalel School at Jerusalem, several faded bits of parchment which grandfather lifted reverently and tried to read, paper cutters and penholders made of olive wood. Last of all, he placed in Judah's hands a little book with wooden covers. "This is your Chamishah Osor present," said Mr. Abrams. "I bought it in Jaffa. The pressed flowers inside grew in Palestine and the covers are made of olive wood."

A ray of sunlight pierced the gray storm

clouds outside and shone upon the little wooden-bound book in Judah's hand. It seemed to warm the heart of the olive tree into life again and it stirred beneath the kindly light and the touch of the child's loving fingers. It was not aware of the strange room, the old man who bent over the Hebrew parchments, the young traveler who stood beside him. The polished bit of olive wood saw only that the child who held it in his hand was round-cheeked, with merry dark eyes and a laughing mouth.

"Was this once a real olive tree growing in Palestine," said Judah, "and may I really keep it?"

"Yes. And every time you look at it, don't forget that 'way over there our colonists are planting olive trees and helping the land to bloom again for other people—just like the old man in Rabbi Choni's story."

"When I'm a man," promised Judah, "I'm going to Palestine and plant trees, too."

"I always knew my little brother Gideon would come back," murmured the heart of the olive tree, as it fell into a long sleep, for it was very tired.

THE PURIM PUSSY

Marion sat curled up in one corner of the sofa, thinking hard; the Queen of Sheba, as her name happened to be that week, sat curled up on Marion's knee, also thinking very hard; at least, she looked wise, and that is all one can expect of even the most sensible of pussy cats. Marion was ten years old and might have been pretty if it hadn't been for the freckles on her turned-up nose; the Queen of Sheba was distinctly plain, a striped gray kitten whose ears had looked a little moth-eaten ever since she had scorched them through sitting too near the radiator one wintry evening.

"Queenie," said Marion sadly, for she always made it a point to tell all her troubles to her sympathetic little friend, "Queenie, I just don't know what to do about my Shalach-monoth for Ruth next Sunday. You don't know what Shalach-monoth means, do you, pussy?" as the Queen of Sheba stretched herself with an inquiring yawn, "but that's because you haven't lived in a Jewish family very long and never celebrated Purim before. It's an old Jewish custom, and ever since Miss Hirsch, our Sabbath School teacher, told us about it two years ago, we've always taken Shalach-monoth—that means presents—to some poor or sick person on Purim. Year before last the girls in our class took baskets of cake and fruit and a nice smoking jacket to Grandpa Morris at the Old People's Home; last year we brought some presents to poor Mrs. Frankenstein's children; and this year—" but here the pussy cat with a languid switch of her tail jumped to the floor and walked lazily to her favorite spot in front of the radiator, as though the Purim plans of Miss Hirsch's class were no concern of hers.

"I might have known you wouldn't be interested," Marion called after her angrily. "You don't care any more about what I want to do than Aunt Becky does." And Marion walked to the window to stare gloomily into the street, where the lamps were already glimmering through the dusk. "I wish I had somebody real to talk things over with," she thought gloomily.

For the last two years Marion had lived with her Aunt Becky, who had offered her orphan niece a home on the death of Marion's mother. Aunt Becky was kind enough in her way; she saw that Marion had neat clothes to wear to school and Sabbath School, took excellent care of her when she had the measles, and always insisted that she wear her rubbers in wet weather, just as Marion's own mother would have done. But Aunt Becky seemed to forget her own little girl days and was determined that her niece shouldn't be spoiled by what she liked to call "nonsense." Marion had no toys except those her grandfather sent her on her birthdays, and her few books were prizes received at Sabbath School for perfect attendance or good scholarship. She seldom had any pocket money, and as Aunt Becky considered picture shows and children's parties "nonsense," Marion rarely enjoyed such treats with her class mates. Then, Aunt Becky hated to have strange children "cluttering up the house and bringing mud on the carpets," and so Marion did not dare to invite her friends to her home and often would have been very lonely if it had not been for the Queen of Sheba.

The Queen of Sheba when just a little round ball of a kitten, had followed Marion home from school one day; it happened that Aunt Becky felt unusually goodnatured that afternoon and she had actually permitted her niece to keep the tiny creature, although she disliked cats herself and continually threatened to turn the kitten out of doors if she ever caught her stealing steak from the ice box or jumping upon the bed-spread with dirty paws. But the kitten behaved with such perfect propriety that even Aunt Becky had to confess grudgingly that she wasn't much trouble, although she continually complained that the little glutton drank enough milk to feed a half dozen babies! As for Marion, she found the new pet a far better plaything than her newest doll and much more interesting than any of her story books. As soon as she got up in the morning, Marion would run to the basket in the kitchen to see whether Pussy Gray, as she had named her pet at first, was still there; she never forgot to pour out a saucer of milk for her before she helped Aunt Becky prepare their own breakfast; her last act before leaving the house was to pet Pussy's soft gray head, and more than once she hurried home from school, impatient to catch a glimpse of the round little bunch of fur curled up in the parlor window as though expecting her return.

And it was such a delightful worry to find a suitable name for the cat! At first "Pussy Gray" satisfied Marion; then, when she discovered Pussy's cunning trick of darting out her claws as though she meant to scratch you and as suddenly making them velvet again, she called her "Needles" and "Velvet Paws." For a little while, pussy answered to the name of "Florence Hirsch;" then, feeling that her teacher might not like to have a cat named after her, Marion chose a name from her latest prize book, and even caused her aunt to smile grimly by calling "Robin Hood, Robin Hood!" whenever the kitten failed to appear. But the next week Marion's Sabbath School class had read of the visit of the beautiful Queen of Sheba to King Solomon, and Marion, who was not a little proud of her pussy's queenly walk and stately manners, at once re-named her "Queen of Sheba," calling her "Queenie" for short.

Now that Marion had found a suitable name for her kitten at last, one would imagine that her troubles would be over; but here was Purim coming with its question of a suitable Shalach-monoth for Ruth. For the two previous Purims her Aunt Becky had grudgingly given Marion a little basket of her delicious Homon-taschen of which she was not a little proud, for all of Aunt Becky's friends declared that no one else could make such wonderful Purim cookies. But Ruth had been ill for many months, and Miss Hirsch had advised the girls not to bring her any Purim goodies which the nurse might forbid her to eat.

"She wasn't at all strong before she had the fever," Miss Hirsch had told her class, "and now after lying in bed all this time, she is very weak, and, I am afraid, very lonely. It tires her to have too much company and as she isn't allowed to leave her room you can imagine how long the days seem to her. You know that Ruth isn't poor and doesn't need warm clothing or even toys, for her father and mother are able to give her everything she wants. So I want you girls to think very hard just what she would like best and get her something that will interest her and keep her amused."

After class the little girls had discussed gravely what Ruth would like best. They were all very fond of their sick class mate and longed to give her the nicest possible Shalach-monoth; but then, as Fanny Goldstein put it, "how can we buy anything nice enough for a girl who has everything she wants and has more money than any of us, anyhow?" But by the next Saturday, most of the girls had their Purim gifts selected. Fanny was going to send to New York for a blue and gold tea set, "which will make her breakfasts taste better." Fanny's cousin had picked out a lovely set of linen doilies to go with the tea service. Rae intended to bring a picture for the invalid's room, Lilian a Japanese kimona, Irene a hanging basket filled with ferns, and so on. "And what are you going to get Ruth?" Rae asked Marion at last.

Marion flushed hotly. Not for all the world would she tell the girls that she did not have the money to buy something "nice enough" for their sick friend. "I haven't decided yet," she answered calmly, "but it's going to be very nice."

That evening she mustered up enough courage to speak to her aunt. "Aunt Becky," she began timidly, "this year the girls in my class at Sabbath School are going to take a Shalach-monoth to Ruth Davis."

"And I suppose you want me to make you some more Homon-taschen," said her aunt. "As though I didn't have enough cooking to do without making extras for those Davis' who could buy and sell us a dozen times over! Well," jabbing her needle through the stocking she was darning, "I'll put you up a basket of cakes you wont have to be ashamed of—even in front of Mrs. Davis."

"But I can't take Homon-taschen," explained Marion. "Miss Hirsch said that Ruth couldn't eat sweets or rich things. The other girls are all going to buy her something pretty for her room or to use while she's sick."

"The other girls have fathers who make a lot of money to waste on nonsense," returned Aunt Becky grimly. "I don't think I've got any money to spend for presents for Abe Davis' girl. He can buy anything she wants, can't he?"

"Oh, it isn't the present," cried Marion, her lips trembling as she saw how useless it would be to argue with her aunt, "but she's so lonely, being sick in bed so long, that we thought if we could only do something to amuse her—"

"Give her the doll your grandpa sent last month for your birthday," suggested Aunt Becky, "it's as good as new, isn't it?"

"But she has much nicer ones!" protested the little girl. "I haven't a thing in the world she'd care for; she doesn't like to read much, and, anyhow, my prize books all have my name written in them or the date. But if I had a dollar or two I'd buy her some plants for her window box or—"

"Well, I told you I haven't got a dollar or a dime to waste on nonsense," interrupted her aunt. She jerked the ball of cotton which had fallen from her lap and which Queenie had chased under the table. "I never saw such a cat! I wish to goodness you'd give her to Ruth Davis if she needs amusing. The cat ought to amuse her, and I'd be glad to be able to sit around in peace without having that creature climbing all over me!"

Marion bent over Queenie and gently disentangled her from the cotton. Hugging the protesting pussy, who hated to have a pleasant romp interrupted, she carried her to a corner of the sofa in the parlor to help her think things over. It was only a week till Purim, and

Marion realized only too well that there was no hope of receiving help from her aunt.

"And you won't help me either, you bad Queenie," she scolded, as she stared gloomily at the street lamps. "I'm too little to earn money, and I haven't a thing in the world to sell—except you, and nobody would buy you, even if I could do without my kitty," she added tenderly, as Queenie, feeling lonely again, came purring against her legs. "And I do want to get Ruth something nice," she told the kitten, "because it must be hard for her lying all day in bed with nobody to play with. I know I'd have just died of being lonely when I had the measles, if it hadn't been for you." Then she stopped stroking the cat, while her aunt's words came back to her—"the cat ought to amuse her." Why hadn't she thought of that before? Ruth didn't own a cat and nobody would think of bringing her one. Perhaps none of the other girls had ever had a cat like Queenie and realized what a good companion and plaything a clever and affectionate pussy cat can be. Surely, Queenie would be the very nicest present to give her classmate for Purim.

Marion picked Queenie up and rested her cheek against her fur. "Oh, Queenie, Queenie Cat," she murmured. "I don't know how I'm going to get on without you."

Purim came on Sunday that year. The little girls of Miss Hirsch's class, all of them dressed in long cloaks to cover the bright, fantastic dresses they wore, met at Lilian's house, each carrying a neatly wrapped package under her arm. Marion was the last to arrive and she flushed a little as she saw that she was the only one to carry a basket covered with a white cloth.

"It makes it seem more like Purim to carry your Shalach-monoth in a basket," she explained shyly. "Didn't Miss Hirsch tell us that they always used to cover their Purim presents that rich people shouldn't try to show how much they were giving and poor people didn't have to be ashamed of what they gave?"

"Well, I know I'm not ashamed of my lovely tea set," declared Fanny, hugging her long box closer. "It came from New York and—why, isn't there something moving in your basket?" she demanded, pointing to the heaving cloth.

Marion drew her cloak around her gift. "I—I'm not going to tell you until we all get to Ruth's and show our presents," she stammered.

But when they were all gathered in Ruth's sunny bedroom with its pretty white furniture and dainty blue hangings, Marion felt more and more ashamed of her poor gift. How could she give what Aunt Becky had more than once called "a common tramp cat" to Ruth, who could own a dozen Angora pussies if she wanted them? And how the other girls would laugh at her! So she left her little covered basket on a couch in the corner, hoping that no one would ask to see her present, and firmly resolving not to offer her gift until the girls had gone—unless the Queen of Sheba got out and made a fuss.

At first there was too much excitement for any one to notice the absence of Marion's gift. The little girls had all put on the dresses they had worn for the Purim masquerade at Sabbath School, and for a while Ruth was kept busy admiring the pretty costumes, from Emma's long purple robe which made her look like a real Queen Esther to Rae's funny clown dress of red and yellow stripes. Then came the party, and although Ruth could not taste the ice cream in the pretty dishes or the pink and white cakes and candies, she enjoyed this part of the afternoon even more than her guests, for her mother opened the packages one by one and laid the presents on the bed beside her.

Mrs. Davis was just unfolding Elsie's embroidered doilies, when a strange voice sounded above the girls' laughter, a voice that rose from the corner of the couch and repeated "Me-ow," first plaintively, then with all the anger of a spoiled kitten, who, having waked from her nap, wanted to share the merrymaking, too. "Meow!" said Queenie, and she added, although no one but Marion understood her, "Me-ow—let me out at once."

"Why, it sounds like a cat," cried Mrs. Davis.

"I guess it's my present," said Marion weakly, and, flushing to the roots of her hair she pulled the white cloth aside and lifted her Shalachmonoth from the basket. Her friends looked at each other, hardly knowing whether to laugh or not; they might have suspected another girl of bringing her pet kitten to a Purim party for a joke, but they knew that Marion never played jokes and hated teasing. Then, before anyone could speak, Ruth held out her thin little arms for the kitten, crying, "Oh, did you really bring it to me? Let me have it," and a moment later Marion's humble gift sat purring upon Ruth's pillow, lapping up ice cream out of a pink saucer and looking over the company now and then with her most royal air.

"I think she's going to feel at home with you," faltered Marion, and then she realized for the first time just how lonely she would be without her pet.

Three days later Mr. Davis' chauffeur called for Marion in the big car and took her to the house on the hill "to see Miss Ruth and the kitten." Marion found Ruth lying upon the

THE PURIM PUSSY 119

bed with Queenie resting luxuriously upon a silk cushion near by: she recognized it as the sofa pillow Sarah had brought as her Shalach-monoth. Queenie wore a beautiful blue ribbon about her neck, tied in a hugh fluffy bow behind her ear, and looked more like a satisfied, well-fed queen-cat than ever. She allowed Marion to pet her, but was quite willing to leave her lap at Ruth's low call and to curl up for her afternoon nap upon her new mistress's arm.

"I do believe she likes you more than me," said Marion a little enviously, "I've always heard that cats forget their friends right away, but I never believed it. I suppose it's because you give her lots of cream and nice things to eat and blue ribbons."

"No, I think it's because I'm at home all day and can pet her more than you did," decided Ruth. Her face grew very grave. "Mamma said she could see how much you cared for her when you were here Sunday, and she wondered whether I ought to keep her. Do you want her back again?"

"Well—she's only a common every-day cat," hesitated Marion, "and if you get tired of her—"

"Why, I think she's the prettiest cat in the world," exclaimed Ruth indignantly. "Papa said that if you really missed her, I should give her back and he'd buy me some kind of a fancy white cat with a bushy tail, but I like this one much better, because you didn't buy her at a store; she was your very own and you gave her to me. That makes her seem more of a present than if you bought her the way the other girls did their things."

Marion's freckled face was radiant. "Oh, I'm so glad you like her," she cried, "and I do want you to keep her—forever and ever. And, anyhow, I wont miss her very much if you'll let me come and see her sometimes."

"I want you to come to see both of us whenever you can," Ruth answered, "and when I get well and go back to school, we'll take turns keeping her, if you want to." She paused to cuddle the kitten's sleek head against her cheek. "Won't that be nice—pussy?" Then turning back to her guest, "Isn't it funny, you never told me her name and I forgot to ask!"

"Oh, I called her 'most anything," Marion told her. "I called her Queen of Sheba, or just plain Queenie last week, but I was getting sort of tired of that. Let's call her something else."

The two little girls knitted their foreheads in thought while the kitten stopped playing with the fringe on the silk pillow and tried to look wise. "I know!" exclaimed Ruth suddenly, "let's name her after my party. Wouldn't it be perfectly lovely to call her 'Purim?'"

A REAL PASSOVER

Mendel Rabbinowitz could remember at least a half dozen Seders, beginning with those early far off Passovers when he was the youngest as well as the oldest of the children of the house, with the coveted privilege of asking the "four questions." Then sister Rose had learned to lisp: "Why is this night different from all other nights?" aided by frequent promptings from Mendel, who looked forward to the time when Rose would have to give way to baby Simon; for Mendel, like a good many other small boys, had a poor opinion of girls and he felt that Rose hardly deserved the honor, to say nothing of the first chance of hunting for the Affikomon and receiving any present she might care to ask of her indulgent father.

But now those days seemed very distant to ten year old Mendel. Now those wonderful Passover cakes and shiny nuts and sips of sweet wine seemed hardly more than beautiful dreams seen through the heavy clouds that had hovered over Mendel's home ever since father went away to America. To be sure, everything promised well at first, when father wrote long letters about the "golden land," of his work in a shop and his hope to send for mother and the children. "And then," he had written more than once, "then Mendel and Rosie will go to school and learn to be real Americans. We will all be happy here, for in America it is safe to be a Jew."

Mendel had learned all too soon that it was not safe to be a Jew in Russia. Shortly after his father's departure for America, the great war had swept the country, leaving waste and ruin behind it. There was scarcely a man, woman or child in all Europe who was not touched by the horror, but of all those who suffered, Mendel's people had the most to bear. The Jews were mistrusted and mistreated alike by Russians and Germans; those who had been wealthy in times of peace now found it hard to buy a bit of bread; the very roofs were burned above the heads of the unhappy women and children whom the fathers had left behind as they marched toward the battlefields. And, at last, they too went forth, a pitiful army, wandering hungry and ragged along the roads in search of shelter and food. Last Passover had found Mendel, his mother and his little brother and sister living in a cellar with a handful of other refugees. There had been no thought of raisin wine and matzos that year; no singing of the Seder hymns; and, if any of the tired broken people prayed, they did not repeat the old Passover prayers of gratitude for deliverance from Egypt, but entreated the God of their fathers to deliver them from the scourge of war and restore their loved ones who, they feared, they were never to see again.

Almost from the outbreak of the war, Mendel's mother had received no letter from America. Nor could she be certain that the few post cards she wrote, all read and stamped by the censor before they were allowed to pass, ever reached him. She knew how he longed to help them, how he missed the children, Mendel and Rosie and little Simon, whom he had last seen as a baby a few months old; she was sure that he was doing his best to send them the money orders which had come regularly every month ever since he had found work in America. But now neither money nor message came to cheer them as they huddled in their dark cellar and trembled to hear the guns roaring upon the nearby battlefields.

The battle came nearer and nearer. The Germans who had captured the village, were driven out by the Russians and before Passover week was over Mendel had seen and heard such dreadful things that he sometimes felt like one living in a terrible dream. The Jews were accused of aiding the Germans, of acting as spies in order to bring about a Russian defeat. Several old men were shot although they were guilty of no crime except that of being Jews; while the other Jewish refugees were driven out upon the roads, and once more Mendel and his brother and sister were tossed about like tiny paper boats children sometimes try to float upon the ponds in summer-time.

But that was a year ago and now it was Passover again. Mendel's mother and several of her old neighbors had somehow managed to live through the long, dreadful winter, to reach at last the great ship which bore them across the ocean to America. Now they waited at Ellis Island, for they could not enter the new land until some relative called for them and promised them a home.

And Mendel's father had not come! Mr. Boris, the agent of the Immigrants' Society who had visited them, said that he had been unable to locate Mr. Rabbinowitz, who must have left New York during the long interval since his family had last heard from him. He would do his best to trace Mr. Rabbinowitz, he said; but until they heard from him, the family could not take the little ferry boat which would bring them to New York, to a real home in the land of refuge.

A REAL PASSOVER

"You promised that we'd all have Seder with papa this year," Rosie reproached her mother. "I want him to come and get me right away. I want him to get me a new dress and shoes for Pesach and I want to ask the 'four questions' the way I used to at home."

Mrs. Rabbinowitz did not answer her, but her lips trembled. Mendel, who during the last three years had learned to think of himself as the man of the family, tried to divert her and laughed teasingly. "I don't believe you remember a single word in Hebrew," he mocked. "You can't get any further than 'Why is this night?' can you?" and little Rosie had to confess almost tearfully that she could not. "All right, I'll teach you then," Mendel told her condescendingly, "only you'll have to pay attention and learn fast 'cause father might come for us at any time and take us to make Seder with him in New York and you'll want to be ready, won't you?"

Rosie nodded till all her glossy curls seemed adancing. "Hurry up and teach me right away, Mendy!" She cuddled beside him on the long hard bench, too intent upon learning her lesson "before father came" to notice her mother's tears. But Mendel saw and understood. Every little while several "real Americans", as he called them to himself, would come into the long receiving room, crowded with benches on which sat the newcomers from the old world, waiting for their friends and relatives. Then there would be choking sounds, in which he could hardly tell the laughter from the crying, quick exclamations of greeting, long and tearful embraces. No wonder his mother cried as she tried to keep little Simon amused and quiet; for all about them other fathers and husbands were taking their families away, but Mendel's father never came.

"And I thought we'd be with father in New York for Pesach," thought Mendel. "They won't let us in without him and if he doesn't come at all—" but Mendel did not dare to think about that. He was only a little boy, but he was old enough to understand what Mr. Boris had told his mother. What would happen to them if father never came and they were not allowed to enter the beautiful new world! And they were so near, too! Why, at night he could see the light flashing in the great hand of the tall stone woman standing in the harbor. Jake, one of the workers on the Island, told him that she was called "Liberty"; that the French people had given her to the United States long ago and that year after year she stood there, her light welcoming all the wanderers who came to find a home in free America.

"I don't know much about pictures and statues and those things," Jake told Mendel one day, "but I like her a lot." Jake had asked Mendel to take a walk with him during the noon hour and now they stood on the edge of the pier looking across the shining waters that lay between them and the white towers of New York. Mendel, who had been gazing wonderingly at the red brick buildings which sheltered the immigrants on the Island, the hospital for the sick among them a little apart from the rest, turned back to Jake who had given him his first opportunity of exploring his strange surroundings. These buildings, the great white statue, the many towers across the harbor, all seemed very wonderful to the boy, but none quite so wonderful as his new friend. For Jake Holzberg, although a Jew, was just like other "real Americans" and had been allowed to go through school and could travel all over the country, he said, without a passport, and could even have opened a store or practised as a dentist had he wanted to. Visitors to the Island saw in him only a lanky young man with a heavy shock of hair and small twinkling eyes; but Mendel firmly believed that Jake was a most unusual person, as he was permitted to roam all over the Island, to say nothing of returning to the enchanted city of New York every evening. As he walked about with Jake that warm April day it seemed almost as if the tall buildings across the waters, and even the great white statue, belonged to the young boy who pointed them out to the little stranger.

"Yes, I like that statue a lot," Jake repeated. "I wasn't much older than you when I came to America and I guess I remember the lady with the light better than anything else about that time. I didn't know what I was getting into then, any more than you do; but I knew what I was leaving behind—just like you. You see, my folks were killed in Kishiniev: shot down just because they were Jews. And I didn't know how it was going to be here. But my uncle took me over the ferry to New York and the next week I was in school and feeling like a genuine American."

"And weren't they ever mean to you for being a Jew—like over there?" Mendel marveled, for it was hard to believe that all the good things Jake told him could be true.

Jake threw back his tousled head and laughed. "It doesn't make a difference here," he told Mendel. "You'll find America's a good place to live in, all right. I'd rather be a street cleaner in little old New York than one of those kings or dukes over there in the old country. You just see how you're going to enjoy going to school and living in America."

"But I don't know if we're ever going to get a chance to be Americans," answered Mendel wistfully. "You had your uncle to come after you, but we've got nobody but father and if he doesn't come and get us, they won't let us in, will they?"

"Don't you worry, sonny," Jake assured him, trying to appear more hopeful than he felt. "Mr. Boris says he's doing all he can to find your dad—he told me so himself. And while you're waiting for him, they're treating you pretty nice here, aren't they, so what are you fussing about?"

"It's nice to have a place to sleep," Mendel admitted. "Last winter we slept in cellars or barns or any place we could find and it was dreadfully cold. And I like the good things they give us to eat, too. The cook lady in the kitchen can't talk Yiddish, but when Rosie and I come in there before dinner she always gives us a big piece of bread and butter and we're never hungry anymore. But," he tried to keep his voice from trembling, "I don't want to stay here. I want to live in a real house the way we did before the war. As soon as we got on the ship, mama said: 'Thank God, we will all be together this Passover.' But it's just three days now till Passover and if papa doesn't come for us we can't have a Seder."

He blinked hard to keep the tears from his eyes and Jake was considerate enough to treat him like a man, instead of petting and comforting him as he might have done Rosie. "And suppose he don't come," he said cheerfully, "won't you be all right here over Passover?"

"But we haven't had Seder for three years and I wanted——"

"Didn't you know we had Seder here for all the Jews who can't get ashore before Passover?" Jake asked him. "Some people over in New York send matzos and fruit and chickens and things and we have the finest Seder you ever saw in your life. They never let you bring wine on the Island any other time, but on Passover it's all right, and we have the blessings and the prayers and all that."

"And somebody to ask the 'four questions'?" cried Mendel.

"Sure! If you know them, I'll speak to Rabbi Morris who always arranges things and ask him to let you say them. They always pick out a little fellow and I guess it would tickle your mother," he ended kindly.

"I know them backwards," bragged Mendel. "And I can say them just as fast as the chazan used to read in our schul on Friday night." Then the joy died out of his eager face as he glanced toward Rosie sitting beside her mother.

A REAL PASSOVER 131

Some visitor had given her a doll and the little girl sat nursing it as she crooned a Yiddish lullaby she had often heard her mother sing to Baby Simon:

"Close your eyes, quickly;
Go to sleep, baby dear;
Sleep for a little while—
Supper is here."

It was just like Rosie to be playing with a foolish doll instead of worrying like him and mother, Mendel reflected bitterly. Rosie never worried; she took it for granted that father would come and that she would ask the "four questions" at their own Seder. And if father didn't come, she would most likely enjoy Seder on the Island, especially if she were chosen to ask the questions and could say them nicely. But Mendel knew that one thing would make her unhappy; if he were chosen and she would have to sit silently by. It was not easy for Mendel even to think of refusing such an honor. He already saw the long table with the detained immigrants around it, the visitors from New York, the "real Americans," looking on. He knew how proud his mother would be, for he was sure that he could recite the hard Hebrew words much better than Rosie, and he was certain that his father would be delighted to hear that he had not forgotten, although it had been so long since Mendel had recited them at their own table. Then he remembered his father's farewell to him—although it seemed many years ago, Mendel could recall every word— "Be a good boy, Mendel, and take good care of mama and the children while I'm gone." A lump rose in Mendel's throat. He had tried to take good care of them, especially Rosie. He thought of the dreadful days along the road, when she was so tired that he had carried her in his aching arms until she was able to walk again, the days when she had cried for food and he had always given her the biggest portion of the scanty bit of bread mother told him to divide between them. Rosie was so little and weak that it seemed necessary to take care of her; but, surely, he wouldn't have to keep giving up to her now, when she had plenty to eat and even a doll to play with! His voice trembled a little as he turned back to Jake—

"I'd like to get the chance to ask 'em, unless father comes and takes us away before the Seder," he said.

But the very next morning Rosie came to him for her regular lesson. "Hear me say it, Mendie," she pleaded. "You won't have to help me once." And she rattled off the four questions so easily that even her critical brother had to confess that she "did them pretty well."

"You're doing much better than yesterday," he told her grudgingly.

Rosie flushed delightedly, for Mendel seldom praised her. "I said it all over to my dolly about a hundred times after I went to bed last night," she explained. "And this morning I said it all to Simon while you were going around with Jake. And I didn't make one mistake, did I, Simon?"

Simon, a thin-faced youngster with big eyes, nodded obediently. He dragged his feet a little as he walked and never cared to play with Rosie. Perhaps the hardships he had known from the time he was little more than a baby, had left him so weak and languid. At that moment, Mendel, who was in anything but a pleasant humor, was inclined to be crosser than ever at Simon's spiritless manner. Wasn't it hard enough not to know where his father was, he asked himself, without being bothered with a silly sister (who recited her lesson to a doll!) and a little brother too weak to play with him? It's lucky he doesn't know any Hebrew or he'd expect me to give up to him the same as Rosie and let him say them at the Seder, he thought, crossly.

"Won't papa be glad when I say every word right?" Rosie continued happily. "And maybe he'll show me where he hides the matzah and he'll give me anything I want when I find it. I'm going to ask him to get me a new doll to be a sister to Becky," she told Mendel so confidently that he just hadn't the heart to tell her that father might not be with them at the Seder.

"Who's papa?" asked Simon suddenly.

Mendel, about to laugh, checked himself. His mother had joined the little group in time to overhear Simon's question and her face twisted with grief.

"Who's papa? Do I know him?" Simon asked her.

"I guess you've forgotten him," Mendel answered quickly. "You were just a little baby when he went away. But he's going to come for us soon and bring you a little toy horse and Rosie a doll and mama a new shawl and me——"

"He may never come for us," Mendel's mother spoke quietly, but the boy realized that she had given up all hope. "It would have been better if we had all died over there than come here to wait forever." She broke off suddenly and sat down on one of the benches, drawing her shawl over her face. Simon climbed into her lap, wondering to see his mother cry; while Rosie stared at her with unbelieving eyes. But Mendel drew her aside.

"She'll be all right soon," he told his little sister. "Just go on playing with that crazy Becky doll of yours and pretend not to notice her."

But Rosie, who was a wise little body for her six years, was not so easily diverted. "Why did she say papa wasn't coming for us?" she asked, a trifle anxiously.

Mendel shifted uneasily. "I guess she's worried and gets tired of waiting sometimes," he explained.

"But she said he wasn't ever coming. O Mendie," she stared at him with frightened eyes, "won't he ever come and take us home for Seder?"

"He—he may be a little late getting here," Mendel hesitated. "You know America's an awfully big country—Jake told me—and if they don't find him in New York, he mayn't get here until after Passover."

"But I've learned all my 'questions,'" wailed Rosie. "And if he doesn't take us home for Seder, I can't say them." She turned to run to her mother for comfort, but Mendel held her back. It seemed that although the long journey was over and there was plenty to eat, he still had to take care of mother and the children and "be good" to Rosie.

"Now don't start your crying," he told her

almost roughly. "You're not a baby like Simon and you can't have everything you want. Maybe father will get here in time for Seder, but if he doesn't we can have our Seder here just as well as not."

"But mama can't make a Seder, can she, and you're not old enough," objected Rosie.

"Jake told me they have one every year for people who can't get over to New York before Pesach," explained her brother. "They have wine and matzos and everything just the way we did at home. And a rabbi to read the prayers and things and—" he paused impressively, "the smartest little girl they can get to ask the 'four questions.'"

"I know—that's me," Rosie positively squealed with delight. "I know 'em—you said I did—and you'll ask Jake to let me say them, won't you?"

"All right. Only you mustn't get scared if there are a lot of people there. Now go over and tell mama and I'll try to fix it up with Jake," promised Mendel rather importantly.

On Seder night the great dining room at Ellis Island was blazing with lights and hung with flags. About the tables, with their snowy white cloths, sat men, women and children from every corner of the earth. During the past three years they had lived in one or another of the countries at war; many of them had bled on battlefields for nations that had despised and persecuted the Jews; but tonight they sat together, natives of Turkey and Belgium, of Germany and Morocco, of Palestine and Poland, enemies no longer but bound by the blood ties of the brotherhood of Israel. They felt that all their old hatreds and doubts were to be forgotten forever as they gathered under the American flag which gave them all freedom to celebrate their old, old feast of deliverance from Egypt.

Mendel glanced down the long table with contented eyes. Everything was just as he remembered it at home: the three matzos covered with a napkin, the glass dish containing a lamb bone, a bit of parsley and root and a boiled egg, a bowl filled with a reddish mixture, which his father had once told him was called haroseth and represented the mortar the Hebrews had been forced to make while slaves in Egypt. Mendel noticed, too, the great silver goblet of wine, which he had been told is always set aside for the prophet Elijah. He knew that Elijah visits every Seder table on Passover eve and that the chair piled high with cushions at the rabbi's right hand was for the welcome guest, the friend of the Jewish people who will some day come to announce their eternal freedom. As he thought of all this, Mendel wished heartily that he was little like Simon or a girl like Rosie: it would have helped so much to be able to have a good cry. The old stories brought back his father so very vividly, his father who would have been so proud of Rosie tonight, who, Mendel felt, might have been proud of him, too, for giving Rosie her chance. Why, Jake had told him she would even be asked to open the door to let Elijah in. He remembered how in the old days he had always jumped up joyfully at his father's nod, to unlatch the door for the prophet. In those days he was always sure that he would see Elijah himself—dressed in a long rough cloak and leaning on a staff, just as the rabbi in Cheder had described him. In those days, too, Mendel had believed that Elijah would bring him anything he wanted, that is, if he had been a good boy and had studied his lessons in Cheder, to say nothing of helping mother about the house. Although he felt very grown up now, almost a man and the head of a family, he found himself wishing that he might open the door for Elijah, half believing that he would really catch a glimpse of the old man before he passed.

"And I'd ask him to send father for us soon," thought Mendel, "that next year we could have Passover together."

Rabbi Morris had started the service. He

was a tall, broad-shouldered man with a heavy black beard; his eyes smiling below his little skull cap seemed to embrace every one at the table, before they came back to where Rosie and Mendel sat beside him. Jake had told Mendel that the rabbi had no children of his own; perhaps that was why he had petted Rosie so much before the Seder began and given her a pair of bright-red hair ribbons. Even now Rosie was patting and pulling them into a perkier bow above her curls, in spite of her mother's frown of disapproval. Being a very little girl she was almost as excited over her new ribbons as at the prospect of asking the "four questions".

"Roschen, you will spoil your ribbons—keep your hands down," warned her mother.

"And stick your doll under the table," whispered Mendel. "I don't see why you brought it along for, anyhow?"

Rabbi Morris turned a page of his haggadah. "Now, daughter," he smiled at Rosie, "stand up that everybody may hear you and ask me the 'four questions.' "

Rosie, still clutching her doll, rose to her feet. Her cheeks were as flushed as her ribbons; her free hand clung desperately to Mendel's coat sleeve. "I'm afraid," she faltered, "I'm going to be afraid."

Mendel looked stern. "Go ahead," he whispered, hoarsely, "or—" making the most severe threat he could think of at that moment— "or I'll say them myself. Begin— 'Why is this night—?' Now go ahead!"

"Why is this night different than any other night?" began Rosie, her voice shrill with nervousness, but growing calmer as she went on with the old questions which the youngest child asks in Hebrew on the eve of Passover. She went on bravely, asking why matzos instead of leavened bread were served, why bitter herbs were eaten, why the rabbi reclined upon the cushions of his chair instead of sitting upright as at other meals. And Rabbi Morris answered each question in the old Hebrew phrases, explaining that Passover was a memorial of the deliverance of the Jewish people from Egypt; how, since the bitterness of slavery was over, every Jew might lie upon cushions like a prince as he ate of the unleavened bread his fathers had eaten when they journeyed into freedom.

A murmur of applause arose as Rosie sank back into her seat. "I didn't leave out a word," she told Mendel in a triumphant whisper. "But why is mama crying?"

"I guess it's because she's so proud of you," he whispered back. "Now sit still and listen

A REAL PASSOVER 143

it's Elijah!" thought Mendel, his hand trembling on the doorknob.

But his face clouded with disappointment as he recognized Jake. The young fellow flashed a smile at him before he turned and pointed over his shoulder. "I got him," he said briefly. "Come right in, Mr. Rabbinowitz, and I'll get you a seat so we won't make any fuss and disturb the Seder. Here, kid, be quiet"—for Mendel, unheeding his warning, forgetful of the many strangers waiting at the tables, pushed past Jake and flung himself into his father's arms.

"Papa, papa," he cried, "I knew you would come for us."

He said no more, for Mrs. Rabbinowitz had started to her feet with a wild cry of recognition. She hurried to her husband's side carrying little Simon in her arms, while Rosie, awakened by all the tumult, stumbled sleepily after.

"Is it time to open the door for Elijah? Is that him?" she asked Mendel, rubbing her eyes and pointing to the stranger at the door.

Mendel laughed rather doubtfully. "You silly thing," he chided her, "I knew papa right away and you didn't remember him at all."

It was a little hard to go on with the Seder after that, for among those about the table were many men and women still waiting for missing ones who might never come for them. But at last, Rabbi Morris, with tears trickling down his kindly face, opened his haggadah and prepared to complete the service.

So it was not until the next day that Mendel heard why his father had been so long in coming. Then Mr. Rabbinowitz told his family how two years before he had gone to South Carolina and opened a little store, gradually losing touch with his New York friends, although he had never ceased trying to learn the whereabouts of his wife and children. Only two days before he had received a telegram from the Immigrant Society that had traced him at last. Jake, knowing how much it would mean to all of them not to delay their meeting even until the next day, had promised the society's agent to meet Mr. Rabbinowitz at the train and had brought him straight to the Seder.

"You should have heard how nice I asked the 'four questions,' papa," Rosie told him as they stood waiting for the ferry to take them over to New York.

Her father patted her head, but he looked smilingly toward Mendel. "Mama told me all about it," he assured her, "and I was very proud of my little girl. And when Jake brought me over here last night he told me something

A REAL PASSOVER 145

that made me just as proud of Mendel. It was a fine thing, Mendel, to let her say them instead of you."

"It wasn't much," Mendel mumbled, but he felt very happy.

Rosie didn't understand just what they were talking about, but she guessed that Mendel had been good to her and wanted to thank him. Although she knew he hated to be kissed, she cuddled up to him and tried to pull his face down to hers. "You're a nice boy, Mendie, to teach me the questions, and I want to thank you," she told him.

Mendel saw that his father and mother were talking together and that the other immigrants who were to leave the Island with them did not seem to take any notice of their little group. Feeling unusually tender toward Rosie, he bent down and kissed her. She lifted her stupid doll to his mouth and smiled innocently. "Kiss my dolly, too," she commanded.

But Mendel felt that he had done enough. "We can get on the boat now," he said abruptly, as he helped his father with the luggage. Across the shining harbor he could see the tall white towers of New York; they seemed to smile a welcome to the wanderers. "I'm glad I'm going to live in America," Mendel said to himself as he led his little sister over the gang plank.

THE BOW THAT WOULD NOT BEND

A Lag B'omer Story

Myer liked his Uncle Harry better than all his other uncles, for Uncle Harry, although he was so tall and strong, was very much of a small boy at heart. He knew that little boys like Myer are fond of candy, and always had his pockets stuffed with sweets whenever he came to visit Myer's parents. He guessed, too, that small nephews prefer books about Indians and African hunters to the volumes of Bible stories and useful presents his other uncles are likely to give him; and, since Uncle Harry had traveled "all over the world," or, at least it seemed so to Myer, he was able to tell him the most wonderful stories of cowboys and Indians and of the time a bear had chased him and almost got him, too! No wonder, then, that Myer loved this splendid uncle so much and could hardly wait for his visits.

On a certain spring day, Uncle Harry arrived unexpectedly with three bags of candy and the finest present he had ever brought his nephew: a little Indian suit, feathered headdress, strings of colored beads, and, best of all, a bow of shining wood with three red-tipped arrows. Myer gave a whoop of delight when he saw the bow and arrows, but when he tried to pull the string he found that try as he would he could not bend the heavy bow.

"Are you holding it right?" asked Uncle Harry, who was sitting on the porch smiling like a boy over his nephew's delight in the new toys. "See, this is the way." He deftly fitted an arrow and sent it skimming across the grass. Perhaps he meant to hit the big willow tree just beginning to show its delicate green leaves; instead he grazed the family cat who had come out on the steps to see the fun. Pussy gave him an indignant look, then, more frightened than hurt, ran yowling to the fence where she sat eyeing him with an injured expression for the rest of the afternoon.

Myer couldn't help laughing at kitty's discomfiture, but he grew suddenly sober as he looked over the bow. "I'm afraid I'm not strong enough to pull the string," he admitted, ruefully. "I can pull Dan's all right. Why didn't you bring me a smaller one?"

"That's not very polite," reproved Myer's mother from her porch chair, but Uncle Harry had to admit that he deserved a scolding.

"I liked the looks of it," he confessed, "and I guess I forgot you were only seven and got

THE BOW THAT WOULD NOT BEND 149

you mixed with your cousin Marcus in New York. He's so much bigger than you, and—"

"I'm a big boy, too," asserted Myer, a little indignant. "I—why, I can fight Dan and every boy in my room at school," he ended, boastingly.

"You wouldn't think he was a big boy if you knew how lazy and careless he gets sometimes," scolded Myer's mother, who seemed to think it might do him good to be made to feel a little ashamed before his favorite uncle. "You know we haven't a Sabbath School here because there are so few Jewish children in Mandelville and we have old Mr. Delson give Myer a Hebrew lesson twice a week. And I've heard our 'big boy' say that Hebrew's too hard to learn and he wishes he could wait till he was older."

"Well, it is hard," protested Myer, "and it seems he's always coming just when I want to go somewhere with Dan or play with the boys. But I don't have to take a lesson this afternoon, do I, mama?" he coaxed. "Let me skip one this week and stay and talk with Uncle Harry."

But his mother shook her head smilingly and at four that afternoon Myer, feeling very much abused to have to sit studying Hebrew when he wanted to be walking with Uncle Harry, opened his book with a scowl and made up his mind that if he ever grew up, he'd never look into another Hebrew book—no, sir! he'd go west with Uncle Harry and shoot Indians. He reached across the table for his precious bow and arrows which he could not trust out of his sight. If he were only big enough to use them now!

When old Mr. Delson entered the room a few moments later, a smile crossed his kindly, wrinkled face as he picked up the great bow and examined it. "So it is almost Lag B'omer," he said, more to himself than to Myer. "And the children already have their bows and arrows."

But Myer did not understand. "What have bows and arrows got to do with Lag B'omer?" he asked.

"When you have your lesson," began the old man, but Myer was only too glad to have a chance to listen instead of reciting the passages he had prepared so poorly.

"Please tell me a little about Lag B'omer first," he pleaded. "Is it a Jewish holiday? Why did my bow make you think of it?"

Mr. Delson smiled and a wistful look crept into his faded eyes. "In America the boys and girls do not know when we have Lag B'omer," he said, almost sadly, "but when I was a boy over in the old country—" he leaned back in his chair, his white beard sweeping his breast, his eyes looking far away.

THE BOW THAT WOULD NOT BEND 151

"And you used to keep Lag B'omer over there?" Myer prompted him.

"Yes. It came in the spring time just when we Cheder boys were so glad to run away from our books. We were not like little American boys who want to study all the time and never like vacations," he teased his pupil. "It came between Pesach—(ah, we have no such Seders in America!)—and Shabuoth; it was the thirty-third day of the days when we used to count the omer in Palestine. You remember I told you all about it, Myer?"

But Myer had to confess that he had forgotten.

"When we had our own country and our own Temple," went on the old man, "we used to offer up our omer of barley—about seven pints the way we measure grain nowadays. These 'omer days' became sad ones for our people, who never forgot a dreadful plague that carried away many of them during that season. But there is a story that this plague stopped on Lag B'omer because the pupils of Rabbi Akiba prayed that the people might be spared. So during the dark 'omer days' our teacher picked out Lag B'omer for the 'scholars' holiday.' On that day they permitted marriages which were forbidden during the rest of the seven weeks between Pesach and Shabuoth; and they used to give their pupils a long holiday and take them into the fields to remind them that once the Jewish people were free and had fields and woods of their own. It is an old, old custom and yet even today my little grandsons in the old country are looking forward to their holiday on Lag B'omer and are making bows and arrows to carry when their teachers take them out into the fields."

"But why must they carry bows and arrows?" persisted Myer.

"Some people say it is to remember Simeon ben Yohai. When the Romans conquered Palestine, he had to live in a cave for fourteen years; if they had found him they would have put him to death for teaching the Law to the Jewish people. The story says that he died on Lag B'omer and that at his death the rainbow, which had not been seen during his life, appeared again in the sky. Simeon ben Yohai had said that before the Messiah came to free the Jewish people from their enemies a great bow of many colors would appear in the heavens; so whenever they saw the school children carrying toy bows shaped like the rainbow, it gave them hope that some day a great leader would come again to lead them in battle like Rabbi Akiba and Bar Kochba."

"Was Rabbi Akiba a soldier?" asked Myer

wonderingly. "I thought rabbis were old men who just studied and taught people."

"He was one of the bravest soldiers we ever had," answered Myer's teacher warmly. "Although the Romans forbade all the rabbis to teach the Jewish law, he kept on instructing his pupils until he was thrown into prison. There he was put to death by cruel tortures, and when they wondered to see him bear his sufferings with a smile, he said: 'Every day of my life I have repeated the Shema. Today for the first time I feel what it is to love the Lord my God with all my heart and all my soul and all my strength. That is why I rejoice in all my pain.' Yes, he knew how to fight for the Law although he was not a real soldier. And he did all he could to persuade soldiers to follow Bar Kochba, for he believed God had sent him to deliver the Jewish people from the Romans." He opened his book, but Myer equally anxious to postpone his lesson and hear about the "real soldier," stopped him.

"Please, Mr. Delson," he coaxed, "tell me about Bar Kochba, too. I know mama will want me to know all about Lag B'omer and I like stories better than my regular lessons."

"Then a little holiday because it is almost Lag B'omer," smiled the indulgent teacher. "Only I expect a very good lesson next time!

It would take too long to tell you all about Bar Kochba, but some day when you know more Hebrew you will read all about him yourself. A good many people thought, like Rabbi Akiba, that his name meant 'son of a star' and they believed he would be a Star of Hope to the Jewish people and make them free again. But after he had failed to help them and shown himself a weak and wicked man, those who had trusted him changed his name to 'son of a lie.'

"How could he be a great soldier if he was a 'weak man'?" demanded Myer.

"He was a brave leader and was strong enough to fight lions and hurl great stones; there are a great many stories of his physical strength; but he wasn't strong enough to control his own evil nature and there are other stories which show why the people soon learned to fear and mistrust him. And so he died without bringing us our freedom and the Jewish people knew that they would have to wait a little longer before their real Messiah came to lead them out of slavery." He rose heavily. "Sometimes we grow tired of waiting; but on Lag B'omer when we hear the children laughing and playing in the fields, it is not so hard to hope. Some day one of these children may become a great soldier for our people." He gathered up his books. "I see your father

THE BOW THAT WOULD NOT BEND 155

coming down the street, so it must be late. Have a good lesson next time and don't forget what your bow means when you play with it," he smiled as he went down the path.

"I wonder what he meant by boys growing up to be soldiers for the Jews," thought Myer as he watched the bent old man passing through the gate. He picked up his bow lovingly. "If a man like Bar Kochba would come around again, Dan and Uncle Harry and I would help him fight!"

That evening Myer, who had listened open-mouthed to Uncle Harry's tales of his adventures in the west, went upstairs to bed very reluctantly, carrying his precious bow and arrows with him. He laid them on his pillow, smiling to think what great fun he and Dan would have when they set up a target in the back yard and learned to shoot "just like Bar Kochba and his soldiers." The boy was very tired, for it was past his usual bedtime; yet when he was once in bed, he could not fall asleep but lay dreamily watching the moonlight as it streamed through the open window and flowed like a silvery stream across the bow and arrows lying upon the pillow. He began to think of the stories Mr. Delson had told him; with his half-closed eyes he seemed to see the old man sitting beside his bed, his wrinkled face glowing with pride as he told him the stories of Akiba and Bar Kochba. Myer wondered why his teacher's voice seemed to come from such a long distance—far, far off—until he couldn't hear it any more—only the sound of rushing waters and the murmur of swaying trees. Slowly he opened his eyes to find himself beside a foaming stream that dashed between the rocky banks. All around him were great trees, swaying sadly in the wind, while the place was filled with a dim light that was neither of the sun nor the moon, and he became afraid.

Then, as Myer stood trembling beneath the great trees, he saw a strong young man as tall and broad-shouldered as his Uncle Harry, striding toward him, and he felt that the stranger must be Bar Kochba. The hero carried a great bow; he did not speak as he came to Myer, but, thrusting the bow into the boy's hand, signed to him to try to draw the string. Myer tugged with all his might, but he was not strong enough to pull it, and he cried bitterly, for the tall man seemed very angry as he snatched his bow away and disappeared among the trees.

But in his place stood an old man with a beautiful long white beard which made him look strangely like old Mr. Delson. He carried no weapons, only a scroll such as Myer had seen his own grandfather read when called up to the reader's desk in the synagogue. The old man opened the scroll before him and Myer timidly read the Hebrew words he never had been able to read before: "Blessed be He who gave unto His people the Law in His holiness." Then the old man spoke gently:

"Why were you weeping, my son?"

"I couldn't pull the string of Bar Kochba's bow. I am afraid I will never be strong enough to fight," Myer answered.

The old man smiled. "Nay, for I also fought for my people though my arms were weak with age. Do not grieve, little son, for did you not show me just now that you are already learning to use the greater weapon of our people? The bow of Bar Kochba will never be strung again, for we are indeed a people of peace. But the Law for which I and my brethren suffered and died will endure forever; and this Law you must learn diligently and love with all your heart and with all your soul and with all your might."

As he spoke a great light seemed to shine from the Torah he carried, and fill the place. The light fell on the bow upon the pillow and across Myer's face; he opened his eyes to find himself in his own little bed with his mother bending over him.

"I thought the sunlight would wake you up when I pulled the curtains," smiled mother. "What a lazy little boy! Hurry and get up or you'll be late for school. There's no use pretending to be half awake," she added severely, as Myer lay blinking stupidly at the sunshine. "I know you had a good night's sleep."

But Myer knew better!

CLOTHES

A Shabuoth Story

The girls of the Confirmation class of Temple Emanuel sat in the vestry room discussing a most important problem. It was just a month before Shabuoth and they felt that they must decide at once just what they would wear for Confirmation. As every girl had ideas of her own and all were equally sure that their suggestions were the best, it was rather hard to come to any decision, although they had been arguing more or less excitedly ever since Rabbi Louison had dismissed the Confirmation class over an hour before.

"Well, we'll all have to look just alike," declared Irene Perlman with her pretty air of decision which made her a born leader among her friends. "I went to my cousin's Confirmation last Shabuoth and the girls wore anything they pleased; why, one of them actually had on tan slippers, and, girls, it was positively awful. We just must decide what we're all going to wear and stick to it."

"I hate white slippers," announced Rae, "they always make my feet look enormous."

"They're the only thing to wear," protested Deborah. "They don't make your feet look a bit bigger if you get nice kid ones."

"But aren't kid slippers very expensive?" asked Marion timidly. She knew that her aunt with whom she lived would object to spending a cent extra on what she liked to call "nonsense." Fortunately, her grandfather had promised to pay for her Confirmation outfit, but Marion thought it safest to be as economical as she could.

"We're only confirmed once in our lives and we have a right to get just what we want," insisted Irene. "Anyhow, it always pays to get the best, mother says, and if we get nice kid slippers we can wear them to dancing school all next winter."

"That will mean silk stockings, I suppose," ventured Deborah. "I guess you're right, though; we ought to have everything just as nice as we can. Only it's going to cost a good deal with long gloves and our bouquets and all that."

"But won't we look just great?" laughed her cousin Frieda. "I'm glad if the rest of you girls decide to get a lot of expensive things; then mama will have to give in and get me what the others have whether she wants to or not. And let's have our dresses made out of

CLOTHES

the same material, too. I think net lace would be lovely."

Here Ida Baum, who had not spoken once during the meeting, stood up and began to fasten her plain little jacket. "I'm sorry I can't stay any longer, girls," she said as she gathered up her Confirmation note book and papers, "but I promised mother I'd be home as early as I could. She isn't very well today and I'll have to help in the store." She turned to Irene. "You can tell me what you girls have decided when you see me at school tomorrow. 'Bye, everybody," and she left the room.

"It's a pity she can't take more interest in things when she's valedictorian," Rae whispered to Frieda.

But Irene had the floor again. "It's no use talking and talking and talking," she said impressively. "As long as we're all sure we're going to have everything alike we may as well vote now on what we want. First, how many want white kid slippers?" Every hand went up, Marion's last of all. "Now for silk stockings." She laughed happily. "Girls, if those horrid boys don't spoil everything, we're going to be the nicest looking class that was ever confirmed in this temple!"

It was almost six o'clock when Irene and

Deborah, who lived next door, walked home together. "I suppose mama will make a fuss when I tell her what we've decided on," Irene said a little doubtfully. "She's always preaching that she hates to see little girls overdressed. Little girls!" She laughed at the thought. "Why, I'm fourteen in July and I could pass for fifteen any day if mama'd let me wear my hair up like Frieda."

"I'm afraid my mother won't like the idea of such a fancy dress either," Deborah answered. "I couldn't say anything about it at the meeting with Marion and Ida right there, but mother was saying the other day that she thought we ought to be very careful not to wear anything for Confirmation that the poorest girl in the class couldn't afford. Only I didn't see how I could say anything this afternoon," she ended doubtfully.

"Oh, anybody can afford what we decided on," Irene asserted easily. "I'm going to have my dress made at Mrs. Breen's—she's very expensive, you know. But the girls who have to save money can get their dresses made at home; and even if the other things are a little high they can save on the rest of their summer clothes. Anyhow, I don't see why you and I have to look shabby because they can't look nice."

CLOTHES

"But if it's going to be hard for Marion and Ida," suggested Deborah a little timidly, for she was always rather uncertain when she opposed Irene in any of her decided opinions. "I know Marion's aunt can afford to get her anything she needs, although she's sort of queer and may make a fuss about it; but I don't see how Ida can afford to fix up like the rest of us. Rae told me that her father's dead and I guess her brother is only a young boy, so he doesn't earn much and they live behind that little store they have right near school. So they must be rather poor; you know yourself that Ida never dresses up for our parties like the rest of us."

"Oh, that's because she's so queer and isn't interested in clothes," decided Irene. "I'm in her room at school and I know her better than you do. She's always got her nose in a book, even at recess. Of course, she gets high marks but I think it's better to have a little fun once in a while. And you know how she listens to every word Rabbi Louison says in Confirmation class. I suppose that's why she stood highest in the examination last week and he made her valedictorian. Only I wish he'd picked out a girl with more style. Now Ruth would have looked too sweet for anything up on the platform and he didn't give her any part but the closing prayer."

They had now reached the handsome apartment house where Irene lived and she hurried up the stairs as she caught sight of her mother waiting for her at the window. "I'm afraid we're awfully late," she called back over her shoulder. "And don't you worry about Ida; I'll fix it up with her at school."

Mrs. Perlman met her at the door. "You're very late, Irene," she chided. "Papa was getting quite worried about you. No, don't stop to tell me what delayed you, but get ready for dinner right away. We were just ready to sit down when you came."

Irene lost no time in washing her hands and face and brushing back the pretty curls which her mother would not allow her to "put up" in a fashionable knot. Then she hurried into the dining room, kissed her father and slipped into her place, too hungry at first to stop eating her soup, even to discuss the matter which was uppermost in her mind. But by the time her plate was empty she was ready for conversation.

"Mother," she began, "do you know there's just about a month before Confirmation and we haven't even started to talk about my dress!"

"There's plenty of time," Mrs. Perlman assured her easily, although a worried little wrinkle appeared between her eyes. She knew

Irene's weakness for pretty clothes and always sensed a struggle when that particular young lady needed a new dress. "I suppose some pretty white dress will do; maybe the one I made you for dancing school last month."

But Irene was perfectly horrified. "Don't you understand that I'll never be confirmed again!" she exclaimed. "Why, it's the most important thing that's ever happened to me— and I've got a perfect record in attendance for the last two years and I'm about ninth in my class, too."

"I think a little girl with a record like that certainly deserves a pretty new dress," commented her father indulgently. Irene was the only child and sometimes he found it hard not to spoil his little daughter.

"I'll need a lot of new things," Irene told him impressively. "New white kid slippers and silk stockings and long gloves. We talked it all over at our class meeting this afternoon and all of us girls decided to dress just as much alike as we could. You know, it would spoil everything if one or two of the girls wore black shoes and stockings and the others didn't."

"But are you sure all the girls in your class can afford to get such an elaborate outfit?" questioned Mrs. Perlman. "Perhaps there will be a few whose fathers can't buy them anything but very simple clothes."

"All the girls said they'd get just what the others did," Irene assured her. "Even Marion, though she never dresses up or goes out like the rest of us. And Ida Baum wasn't there when we decided on everything; she had to go home early. Rae says that her father is dead, but she's got a brother working and I guess she can get what the others do if she wants to," she ended easily.

But the next day at school, Irene felt a little less confident when she told Ida of the plans the girls of the Confirmation class had made for their "outfits." "You remember we all decided to dress alike," Irene explained. "I guess lace net costs a lot; but it always pays to buy something good and maybe we can have these dresses made over when we graduate from high school. Do you think your mother will get you everything?" she ended rather doubtfully, for Ida did look decidedly shabby, not at all like a girl who could afford lace dresses and silk stockings.

"I don't know," answered Ida slowly. "Perhaps, if I tell her that all the other girls are going to dress alike, she'll get me what I need."

"And tell her you'll have to look especially nice, because you're to be valedictorian," urged Irene. "Why, it's going to spoil everything if you don't make a good appearance."

CLOTHES

Ida's plain brown face flushed painfully. Then, realizing that her thoughtless classmate did not mean to be unkind, she answered quietly, "I'll talk it over at home and I guess everything will be all right. Anyhow, I'll let you know tomorrow."

But as she thought over the situation on the way home, Ida was not so certain that everything would be all right. Although she was hardly fourteen, her mother had been nervous and ailing so long that it seemed quite natural for her big brother Ezra to talk over all of the family trouble with Ida and the little girl knew only too well how hard it was for him to pay the rent and the grocery bills, to say nothing of buying new clothes. "But this is something very important," she told herself, "especially as I'm valedictorian. I just can't go in my last summer's white dress and a pair of cheap white shoes. Irene's right; it would spoil everything."

When Ida entered the store, she found her mother sitting behind the low counter, her worried face bent over a letter. "It's from grandma," she explained, "and sister says she's very poorly. I wish I could manage to go to see her this summer. She's almost eighty, you know, and if I wait too long—" she broke off abruptly; but Ida understood. She realized how she would feel if her own mother were old and feeble and wanted to see her before she died. "But Canada's such a long way off," went on Mrs. Baum heavily, "and I know the fare would be dreadfully high, even if I went on an excursion. Don't say anything about it to Ezra. He's such a good boy, it would make him feel bad that he can't send me to see grandma."

Ida promised, a jealous little pain stirring in her heart. No one knew better than she what a devoted son and brother Ezra was; yet it hurt sometimes to feel that her mother depended entirely upon him. "I suppose it's because he gets a good salary and looks after her, while I'm just an expense," she thought bitterly as she put away her hat and jacket. "I wish I were grown up and through Normal School; it would feel mighty good to be a teacher and make enough to help pay the rent and buy my own clothes."

When her mother went to prepare supper, Ida took her school books into the store and while waiting for customers began to study her lessons for the next day. But for once she found it hard to keep her mind on her work. Thoughts of lace net mingled with her history dates; when she tried to concentrate on her grammar lesson, she found her mind wandering to such tantalizing subjects as silk stockings and long

CLOTHES

white gloves. She saw herself dressed in all the Confirmation finery that Irene had told her the girls intended to wear; then smiled grimly as she pictured herself in the last year's white dress she knew her mother expected her to use, without gloves, wearing cheap slippers and stockings. "I can't do it, I just can't do it!" she repeated fiercely. "I'm ugly anyhow and I know the girls all think I haven't any style. So how can I stand up before everybody and make that long speech in my old clothes!"

She was very quiet at supper, but her mother was too absorbed in her letter from Canada to realize that the child seemed worried and absent-minded. As soon as the dishes were put away, Mrs. Baum complained of a headache and went to bed. Ida sat down to finish her neglected lessons and wait for Ezra who was working late and would want a little supper when he came home. It was almost ten o'clock when he sat down to the table, hungry and tired after a long day's work, but not too worn out to notice Ida's troubled manner and to ask kindly: "What's the matter, girlie? Didn't you get on well at school today?"

"Everything's all right there. But it's—it's my Confirmation."

"Well, isn't that all right, too? Aren't you going to be valedictorian?"

"That's the trouble." Hesitating a little, for how could a man understand what a new dress would mean to her, Ida told her difficulties. "I know you think I'm silly," she ended timidly.

Ezra pushed back his empty plate. "Not a bit," he reassured her. "Though I do think the young ladies in your class are pretty foolish for making a lot of trouble for some of you. Why do they want to dress up like a lot of dolls? Anyhow," abruptly, "the trouble's started, and we'll have to see it through. Going to cost much?"

"A great deal," admitted his sister. "I haven't spoken to mama about it, but I know how high everything is just now and—"

"Well, don't say a word to her about it just yet," counselled Ezra. "She's got worries enough. And I've got a little money put away —maybe I can see you through."

"It's all right, mama," Irene cried the next afternoon as she ran into the living room. "Ida told me that we should all wear what we wanted to and that she'd manage not to 'spoil the effect.' Wasn't that a funny way to put it? And when are you going to start on my dress?"

"I think you little girls are very foolish," warned Mrs. Perlman. "I hate to see children

CLOTHES 171

your age dressed in such expensive material. But I'll tell Mrs. Breen to make it very simply."

Irene gave a cry of protest. "It would spoil that lovely lace to make it just like an everyday dress. I saw the prettiest pattern in your magazine the other day," and she ran off for the fashion book. Nor was she satisfied until her mother had reluctantly promised to allow her to have the new dress just as elaborate as the one Irene admired.

Mrs. Perlman took Irene to the dressmaker's several days later and smiled in spite of herself at the child's seriousness. For it was evident that Irene was far more concerned over the drapery of her skirt and the length of her sleeves than anything else connected with her Confirmation. It worried her mother a little, too. Sometimes she feared that the little girl was growing vain and selfish.

On the way home they met Ida, her last year's hat looking painfully faded in the bright May sunshine. She smiled shyly and passed on. Mrs. Perlman looked after her. "What an intelligent face your little friend has," she commented. "Who is she, Irene?"

"That's Ida Baum. I guess she's bright enough—she's valedictorian of our Confirmation class, you know, and get's awfully high marks in school. But she always goes around with such a long face as though she couldn't forget her school work for a minute!"

"I thought she looked a little worried," suggested her mother.

"Oh, she always looks like that," Irene answered lightly. "And maybe her mother's sick again."

By this time Irene's mind was entirely at ease about her costume, but she received a rude shock a few days later when she asked Ida to lend her the broad gold bracelets she had seen her wear to the Confirmation class. "They're so lovely and old-fashioned, I want to wear them when we give our Shabuoth play," Irene explained.

"I can't let you have them," answered the other after a little hesitation.

"I'll take the best care of them," Irene promised. "You can give them to me just before the entertainment and—"

"Oh, I'm not afraid you'll hurt them. But I —I haven't got them any more."

"You lost them? What a shame!" cried Irene with real sympathy, for she had always admired the bracelets.

Ida's honest little face burned crimson. "No. I—needed the money—so I sold them," she ended lamely. "The lady upstairs always liked them and she gave me ten dollars for them.

CLOTHES

I hated to do it because they belonged to my mother when she was a little girl and she gave them to me on my tenth birthday. But I needed the money," she repeated doggedly.

Irene felt she had a right to be indignant. "And she seemed such a nice girl!" she thought. "Just to get clothes like the rest of us she's sold her mother's bracelets. And there I was worrying because I might be better dressed than she was. Now I'll wear what I please."

Mrs. Perlman found Irene a most exacting little person during the next few days. Determined to outshine every other girl in the class with her finery, Irene not only raged over imaginary shortcomings in her dress, but found fault with her new slippers and declared her gloves didn't fit. Then the day before Confirmation, Mr. Perlman caused more trouble by bringing home an exquisite gold chain for Irene to wear with her new dress.

"It's very beautiful," admitted Mrs. Perlman, "but I hate to have Irene wearing jewelry until she's older. This is much too elaborate for a little girl. Wear it when you're in high school, Irene. I'd better put it away for you."

"But I bought it for her to wear now," insisted her father. "And it won't hurt to wear it—just for Confirmation, anyhow."

So the next day a very happy girl gave the

last flirt to her fresh white hair ribbons before she ran to join her friends in the little dressing room at the back of the Temple auditorium. Irene knew that she was pretty; she was sure that her dress was just right; and, best of all, her new necklace was clasped about her throat. Her eyes sparkled with pleasure when her friends crowded about her to admire it.

"You're just a picture," whispered Deborah. "Now if Ida only looks all right everything will be fine; the other girls are perfect, aren't they?"

"You don't have to worry about Ida," answered Irene a little sharply. "I guess she'll look as nice as any of us when she gets here."

But Ida did not come. At last, when the exercises could be postponed no longer, the organist began the opening anthem and the confirmants moved slowly down the aisle. The girls made a lovely picture in their soft white dresses, their hands filled with white rosebuds and even the boys tried not to slouch or walk as though conscious of their new shoes. It was a very beautiful service, all the proud parents and relatives agreed, and, as neither Ezra nor Mrs. Baum were in the audience, there was no one to miss Ida's valedictory. Of course, the girls all agreed that it was very queer she had not come, but then they always expected queer things of Ida Baum! Irene had intended to mention the matter to her mother, but there was company at dinner and guests kept drifting in all afternoon and evening. But the next day at recess she asked bluntly:

"Was your mother sick, Ida, or didn't you get your dress done in time? We waited and waited and we didn't know what to think when you didn't come."

"I guess you got along all right without me," Ida answered dryly.

"But what was the matter?" urged Irene. "I thought you had your dress and slippers and everything ready all the time. Isn't that why you sold your bracelets?"

Ida's gentle eyes fairly blazed and her voice trembled a little. "I'll tell you why I didn't come," she said angrily, "and then I don't want you to mention Confirmation or clothes to me again. I don't need to tell you I'm not rich like the other girls in the class; and yet you expected me to get things I couldn't afford."

"But you said it would be all right," protested Irene faintly.

"I thought it would. Ezra had a little money laid aside and I know mamma would have been glad to have me use it. But two weeks ago my aunt wrote that grandma was much worse;

they thought she was dying. They live way up in Canada and the tickets and everything cost almost as much money as Ezra had in the bank. I didn't want him to do everything for mama; I wanted to do my share, too. And I couldn't have her worried. So when I saw how anxious she was to see grandma again—"

"You sold your bracelets!" interrupted Irene.

"I didn't have anything else. Mama didn't want to take the money, but I made her. And we got a letter this morning saying grandma was a little better and it did her a lot of good to see mama again. I'm glad we sent her; it was worth more to me than all the Confirmations in the world," she ended defiantly.

"But why didn't you come anyhow, even if you didn't get a new dress?" Irene asked, avoiding her eyes.

"I wasn't going after you girls said it would spoil everything if I wasn't dressed like the others. And I guess Ezra's right saying I didn't miss much if Confirmation just means a lot of fussy clothes. But I don't want to talk about it any more," and, her voice breaking into sobs, she turned quickly away. Irene looked after her, her own lips twitching. She longed to comfort Ida, but she was afraid to follow her.

"Father," Irene began abruptly at the dinner table that evening, "how much did you pay for my new necklace? I know it isn't polite to ask, but I just have to know," and, looking not a little ashamed, she told Ida's story to her parents. "And if you'll only take my necklace back to the store, father," she pleaded, "and give me ten dollars, I'll buy Ida's bracelets back for her. I know I couldn't wear it again without thinking how I dressed up like a peacock and kept Ida away, just because we girls didn't think of anything but our clothes."

Her father nodded gravely. "But I'd like the bracelets to be a present from all of us," he suggested.

"And I want Irene to keep her necklace," added Mrs. Perlman. "It may help her to remember how she and the other girls spoiled Ida's Confirmation."

"I don't need to be reminded of it," answered Irene almost savagely. She pushed back her chair. "I'm through with dinner," she said shortly and left the room. There was a suspicious break in her voice and her father seemed about to follow and comfort her, but Mrs. Perlman detained him.

"I'm glad she's unhappy over her thoughtlessness," she told him. "Perhaps it did her good to be confirmed after all. She needed this lesson, but I'm afraid it's been pretty hard on Ida."

THE WESTERN WALL

A Tisha B'ab Story

Israel stood leaning against his scraggy donkey, one lean hand upon the beast's bridle, the other clenched angrily as he watched the group of American tourists approaching the Wailing Place. It was hard enough to have travellers from all over the world spying about his dear Jerusalem, laughing and chattering among the ruins of David's mighty capital; but it always hurt him the most to see a Jew among them. How could the tall young man, who looked as Jewish as the splendid young guards from the farm colonies, stand staring idly at the ruins of the Temple of their people!

Selim, the Arab guide, was telling the story of the Wailing Place at that moment; Israel's lips curved scornfully as he listened to the man's high-sounding phrases. What could Selim know of the real meaning of the Western Wall whose stones had been wet with Jewish tears these weary centuries? Only a Jew could understand why those bent old men stood there wailing and weeping, swaying like mourners in their grief. And yet the tall young Jew with the camera slung over his shoulder looked on the sacred spot as coldly and curiously as did the Gentiles around him.

"It is the one last remaining wall of the Temple of the Jews," Selim was saying in the broken English which Israel had also learned in his dealings with tourists. "The Temple it was destroyed in ruins very many hundred years ago, but those Jews they come here to cry and be sorry and say prayers for Jerusalem."

One of the tourists, a stout red-faced man, laughed contemptuously. "Say prayers for Jerusalem! They don't need prayers here, but an army of street cleaners and a hose or two."

Israel's face burned with shame. It was always that way; visitors in Jerusalem saw nothing but a dirty, broken-down city, where starving Jews huddled together in the shadow of Turkish mosques and Christian missions. If there were only more young men in Jerusalem as fine and strong as the American who was now adjusting his camera! But the young men in Palestine seemed to drift to the Jewish farm colonies beyond Jerusalem, leaving the older folks to weep helplessly before the ruined wall. Israel could hear his own grandfather among them, bent and withered, his white head leaning against the stones as he repeated the mourner's chant in a dreary monotone:

THE WESTERN WALL

"For the palace that lies desolate: We sit in solitude and mourn;

"For the walls that are overthrown: We sit in solitude and mourn;

"For our majesty that is departed: We sit in solitude and mourn;

"We pray Thee, have mercy on Zion! Gather the children of Jerusalem."

The boy's eyes filled with tears as he listened to the old Hebrew lamentation. He had heard the prayer for so many years, ever since his grandfather had brought him to Palestine, a little six year old orphan who believed that Jerusalem was a golden city where David still reigned as king. During the ten years that had passed since the strange pair left their home in Poland, Israel had learned that the majesty had indeed departed from Jerusalem. The Turk ruled in the city of David and where Solomon's Temple had glittered in its glory, hungry old men wept and prayed in vain.

The tourists, eager for new sensations, turned to follow Selim. Only the young Jew with the camera remained behind. Now he unslung it from his shoulder, adjusted the tripod and proceeded to "focus" for his picture, the unconscious group before the Western Wall. Israel watched him, his heart swelling with rage. So the stranger was going to do as so many other tourists had done before: take a picture of the mourners back to his own country for his friends to laugh over as something outlandish and queer. He bit his lips, scowling savagely; if he were only a little taller and stronger, like Haroud from the Petach Tikvah colony, he would teach this hateful American not to make sport of his fellow Jews.

The young man turned and was about to close his camera when he caught sight of Israel, leaning against his scraggy donkey, his fists doubled in helpless anger. As he stood there in the growing dusk, the first breeze of evening fluttering his tattered garments about his lithe brown body, the boy seemed more like one of the Arab donkey boys in the market place than a son of Judah. The stranger found him picturesque enough, "a sulky young Ishmael," as he phrased it, and he hastily adjusted his camera for another picture.

But Israel had seen too many tourists with their cameras not to understand how rapidly the little black box caught one's face. He turned to go, but the stranger called after him.

"Say, come back here," he ordered. Then, as Israel did not reply, but merely tightened his donkey's bridle: "Can't you understand English? I guess you'll understand this, though,"

THE WESTERN WALL

and he pulled a coin from his pocket and held it toward the boy with one hand, pointing to the camera with the other.

Israel had not earned a piaster (Turkish coin, equivalent to about four cents) all day and for a moment he faltered; why not pose for his picture since the money in the tourist's hand would keep his grandfather and him from going to bed hungry that night? He hesitated, and, even as he did so, he heard the camera click and the stranger chuckle at outwitting him.

All of Israel's pent-up anger against the hateful American and his kind, burst into sudden flame. He sprang forward and would have dashed the camera to the ground, had not the young man restrained him and held him at arm's length. The boy chafed and struggled under his strong hand but could not free himself. "Let me go," he cried hotly, speaking Yiddish in his excitement. "I'll not let you have my picture—I'll not let you take it away in your cursed camera."

The young man released Israel, but watched his camera with a wary eye. "You little fool," he said good-naturedly, answering in the same language, "if you're a Jew—and you talk like one—why don't you act like one, too, instead of a wild Bedouin?"

"And why don't you act like a real Jew?" retorted Israel hotly, glad that the man could understand the language spoken in Jerusalem's colony of Russian and Polish Jews. "You come here and make fun of us Jews; you take pictures of old men like grandfather and then you laugh at them—the way that fat man did when he said we ought to clean up a little. Why don't you take pictures of the farm colonies where everything is nice and clean and take *them* back to America?"

The young man looked at him keenly for a moment; then, without a word, he drew a small leather folder from his pocket and opened it before the angry boy. "I took these pictures in Petach Tikvah the last time I visited the Jewish colonies," he answered quietly. "I wanted my friends in America to see what splendid work our young men are doing there. And I am taking their pictures," he indicated the old men before the Wailing Wall, "to show my friends in America how miserable some people are in Jerusalem—how many broken down places there are that we must build up again." He smiled, a bright, boyish smile. "Now do you want to break my camera and destroy my pictures?" he asked.

"But I didn't know—," stammered Israel. "And—and one of those old men is my grandfather."

THE WESTERN WALL

The American's keen eyes softened. "No wonder you were angry when you saw us all staring at them," he answered gravely. "But you see that you were mistaken in me; just as I was mistaken in thinking you an Arab."

"I know I'm as ragged as an Arab donkey boy," Israel answered, flushing a little. "Grandfather can do no work and the money the Halukah (charitable organization for poor Jews in Jerusalem) gives him is scarcely enough to buy him bread. I carry fire wood and sometimes a tourist hires my beast to ride about the city, but we find it hard to live."

"Have you lived here long?"

"Almost ten years. I was just a little boy when grandfather brought me here from Poland. My parents were dead and he could not leave me behind. He had always wanted to come to Jerusalem that he might die in the Holy Land." His voice grew bitter. "And he came to a dead city. But it did not hurt him as it does me. He believes that some day God will send His Messiah to rebuild the Temple and give Jerusalem back to the Jews. He doesn't seem to see the dead things around us —the old men starving, the sick and blind children, the boys like me—," he broke off abruptly.

"The boys like you will rebuild Jerusalem," declared the other slowly.

Israel turned toward him again, his eyes bright with tears. "What can I do?" he demanded, almost savagely.

"Have you ever been to the Jewish farm colonies?"

Israel nodded. "Yes, and many times I have seen the young men from the colonies and once I spoke with Haroud from Petach Tikvah." The boy's eyes kindled with enthusiasm. "He rides like an Arab and the Turks do not scorn him when they meet him in the market place. They laugh at Jews like grandfather and me—they think we can only study and pray; but they know the guards in the colonies are strong and tall and can fight and hold their own."

"Have you ever thought of working in the colonies?"

"I'd rather go to one of them and plant orange trees and ride about on a black horse like Haroud's than do anything else in the world," cried Israel. Then his shoulders sagged hopelessly. "But I cannot leave my grandfather. He is old and feeble—there is no place for him. And he will not leave Jerusalem."

"I leave for Petach Tikvah tomorrow," the young man told him. "I'm an American but I want to try farming in Palestine for a few years. I've got some land there and I want men to work it—men like you who are ashamed of the old Jerusalem and want to build the new one. Here's my card," and he slipped a bit of pasteboard in the boy's sunburnt hand. "If you can get anyone to look after your grandfather, come to see me—donkey and all—and I'll see whether I can't teach you a little about planting and ploughing." He held out his hand and Israel grasped it warmly.

"But you don't know me," he faltered. "You won't do so much for a stranger!"

"All Israel are brothers," quoted the other, "besides I do know you. A lad with your Jewish pride ought to make a good builder. I do hope you can come to me soon. By the way, let me speak to your grandfather and try to persuade him to come with you."

Israel shook his head. "I have tried before—he will not leave Jerusalem. It has been the wish of his heart for so many years to die here that it would be cruel to force him to go away. And I would not tell him of my desire to go to the colonies—he thinks I am contented and it is better that he does not know how I hate my life here."

The boy spoke bravely enough, but in the days that followed his meeting with the American he found it very difficult to overcome the temptation of speaking to his grandfather and begging him to leave Jerusalem. Or, Israel argued with himself, why not leave the old man behind and send him his earnings every month? Ever since he had talked with Haroud, Israel had longed to be a guard in the colonies; he had thought of his ambition as a foolish dream; yet now he had only to go to Petach Tikvah, show the magic bit of pasteboard with the name, *Henry Abrams,* engraved upon it, and he would be transferred from a ragged donkey boy to an independent colonist. But he never dared to speak to his grandfather of his longings, and the old man, who prayed long and earnestly before the Western Wall, never dreamed of the boy's despair.

"Tomorrow is Tisha B'ab (Ninth of Ab)," he told Israel one day. "We must fast as is our custom." He smiled a little. "We seldom eat over much, even when it is not a fast day."

"Grandfather," the boy asked him suddenly, "why must we fast on Tisha B'ab?"

The old man was plainly shocked. "Heathen," he chided the lad, "don't you know that on Tisha B'ab our holy Temple was twice destroyed —once by the Babylonians and once by the Romans? On the ninth of Ab it fell and on Tisha B'ab we fast and mourn for its loss."

Israel moved uneasily. "Yes—I know all that," he answered, "but why must we grieve? It all happened so many years ago."

His grandfather looked at him sharply. "You speak like a heathen," he said sternly. "Though it happened ten times ten hundred years ago, we whose hearts are still Jewish will fast every Tisha B'ab and pray before the Wall."

"It's strange just the Western Wall is still standing," mused Israel.

"Nay, it was the will of God." Unconsciously the old man's body swayed, his voice rose and fell like the old rabbi's in whose Cheder he had heard the legend so many years ago. "When Solomon built the Temple he called upon all the men of Israel to assist him; the nobles built one wall and gave of their wealth; the soldiers another and gave their strength and skill in arms; the sages and teachers gave the third wall and made it beautiful with their wisdom. But the poor and the lowly gave their very hearts to the Holy One, blessed be He, when they labored to rear the fourth wall, which is the western, and that wall remains to this very day and will remain until the Holy One, blessed be He, will send the Messiah, son of David, to rebuild our Temple. Yea, may my eyes behold Thy return," he ended, dropping into Hebrew, and Israel, knowing that he prayed, was silent.

That evening and all the next day Israel sat beside him in the stuffy little synagogue, his heart as heavy as a mourner's, although he often failed to recite the lamentations wailed by those about him. Seated upon the ground like those who weep for their dead, their heads bowed, their eyes streaming with tears, they recited the words of the prophet Jeremiah, who, legend tells us, was an eyewitness of the destruction of Jerusalem by the Babylonians. The hearts of the older men grieved over the destruction of their city centuries ago; but the boy sorrowed at the misery about him and he longed more than ever to escape into the free air of the colonies where he might plant and plough and help to build the new Palestine.

The long day was over at last and Israel's grandfather rose stiffly from his place upon the ground. The memorial candles had burned low in their sockets; outside the synagogue a fiery July sun blazed as it sank to rest. Israel noticed how his grandfather staggered from weakness and caught his arms. Leaning heavily upon his staff, one hand upon his grandson's shoulder, the old man turned homeward.

"You should not have fasted—you look weak and ill," Israel told him.

"From the days of my youth have I fasted on this day; now that I am old shall I disregard His commandments?" reproached the old man, speaking with difficulty.

They came in sight of the Western Wall, last remnant of the Temple, for whose restoration the faithful soul still prayed. Israel urged him not to linger but he would not listen. Staggering a little, he made his way to the Wall, and, pressing his lips against the stones, murmured the heart-breaking chant he had recited so long. "For the palace that lies desolate," he began, swaying to and fro.

"Grandfather," urged Israel, "you have not eaten since yesterday at sunset. You are faint for food. Come home with me."

But the old man did not seem to hear him. "For the walls that are overthrown," he continued to chant hopelessly.

Israel caught his arm to lead him away. Even as he did so, the old man's eyes brightened with a strange hope, his weary shoulders straightened and his voice was like that of a young man. "My eyes shall see His return," he cried triumphantly as he sank to the ground.

When Israel tried to raise him he was smiling as though on the day of fast and lamentation he had indeed seen salvation for Jerusalem. Israel could not weep for him; it seemed a blessed thing that the faithful watcher at the wall had had his wish at last—he had died in his Jerusalem, happy in the thought of the return to Zion. Israel closed his eyes and folded the tired, wrinkled hands. "Good-bye, grandfather," he whispered. He rose, his eyes bright with hope. "I am going to leave Jerusalem but I will come back again and help to build the Wall." He drew the bit of cardboard from his breast; it was soiled and worn with much handling. "I am going to learn to plough and plant," murmured the boy. "When my days of mourning are over I am going to Petach Tikvah to learn to be a soldier for Palestine!"